Sounds Like a Mournful Train Today

By

Kenneth Lee McGee

For Denise

Who years ago gave me
credit for having the courage,
if not the skill,
to tackle a rather
controversial subject.

I would like to thank everyone
who has taken time to visit my website
or my Amazon author page.
I appreciate the support
and kind words.

Thank you Cory Woodward
for the cover photo.

Prologue

"Doug, can you see where you're going? I can't see a thing. This rain is coming down so hard." Barbara Dawson peered through the windshield. "And I absolutely hate thunderstorms."

"It's not that bad, and I've driven this road a million times. We're coming to Bilek's Hill." Douglas Dawson patted her hand to reassure her. "Did you enjoy yourself tonight, Barb? I know you're disappointed Jim and Sarah couldn't come with us."

"I still had a good time," she answered trying to see past the hood of the car.

The lightning flashed again. Followed immediately by a thunderous boom. Doug's night vision momentarily vanished. His heart began racing faster than before.

"That was close! I could feel the wheel shake."

"Maybe we should pull over," Barb said as she glanced out the side window.

Doug shook his head. "We can't. There isn't any shoulder on this stretch of road."

More lightning sizzled through the humid air, and the thunder clapped simultaneously.

"I don't feel good about this, Doug. I've never liked this hill. The road should be wider through here."

"We'll be home soon. You can almost see the town from the top of the hill on a clear day."

Once again the lightning exploded. This time shattering a tree on their left. The thunder reverberated and shook the small compact car.

"That was too close for comfort," Douglas said. He pointed and asked, "Are those headlights on the..."

Chapter One

"Thank you for coming," Florence Jackson said to yet another person offering their condolences. She turned to Sarah McKay and whispered, "Is the whole town here? It feels that way. I've been shaking hands with so many people it hurts."

"You can take a break if you need to, Florence. Jim and I can talk to people," Sarah offered.

Florence shook her head. "Thank you, but I will talk to everyone."

"We will take you home now, Florence," Jim McKay said four hours later. "Sarah took the baby home, and Beth disappeared with friends."

"I need to sit first. I've been on my feet all day." He helped her to the couch. "Thank you, Jim. I wouldn't have made it through the day without you and Sarah."

"We are here for as long as you need."

Florence took a deep breath and ran her hands through her short white hair. "What will I do about baby Caralyn and Beth?"

"We will sort that out later," he assured her.

Barbara Jackson and Sarah Stanfield met in first grade and became instant best friends. Douglas Dawson and Jim McKay met and roomed together for three years at Southern Wesleyan University. While at college the guys met and fell in love with the two best friends. The couples married within days after graduating. Nine months later, Douglas and Barbara welcomed a daughter into their lives. They found jobs and moved to Stockton Woods. For Barbara and Sarah, that meant simply a return to their hometown. In the ensuing years both couples settled into the daily routine of living in the small town of barely a thousand residents. They purchased homes on the same street. Actually, they lived on either side of Florence and Glen Jackson. Barbara appreciated living close to her parents, especially when she welcomed a second daughter into her life.

Stockton Woods had been stunned by the deaths of Douglas and Barbara Dawson in a terrible crash five days before as they returned home from a nighttime visit with friends. All the downtown businesses closed for three hours on the day of the funeral. Stockton Woods was that kind of a close community.

With the ordeal of burying her daughter and son-in-law over, Florence Jackson finally had a moment to sit back and gather her thoughts. She sat on the living room couch with her neighbors, Jim and Sarah McKay, and asked, "What am I going to do with a six-month-old baby and a thirteen-year-old girl, who acts like she's twenty already? I don't have time to take care of them properly unless I quit my job, and I certainly can't afford to do that since I'm five years away from retiring."

"Florence, you know we will help every way we can." Sarah assured her as she patted her hand. "I'm home with Tucker and taking care of a baby is not a burden."

"I'm not too worried about little Caralyn, but Beth is going to be a handful. She is already strong-willed with a mind of her own."

Sarah McKay held the sleeping six-month-old Caralyn Ann in her arms while thirteen-year-old Elizabeth Margaret stayed across town with friends from school. The McKay's three-year-old son, Tucker, scampered about the living room tossing a small nerf basketball in the air trying to impress the baby.

"Beth is taking after her mother. I remember Barbara's rebellious nature when we were that age," Sarah recalled.

"You were both free-spirited and the best of friends," Florence said. *You think you got away with those shenanigans, but I usually knew what you were up to.*

"I am going to miss her so much," Sarah's tears cascaded down her cheek and fell on the sleeping baby.

The silence in the small room, nearly filled to capacity by the couch, two recliners, thirty-year-old end tables and the stand with a TV sitting on top, was broken only by the sound of Tucker's bare feet on the hardwood floor.

After a time, Jim said, "I remember four months ago when we reached that agreement about what we would do in the case of..." He paused as his voice choked and tears filled his eyes. "Sorry... the agreement about... custody... of the kids in case... something... like... this...."

"Daddy, you okay?" Tucker asked as he noticed his father weeping.

"I'm all right, son." Dad wiped his eyes and patted his son's mop of curly, brown hair. "Can you throw me the ball?"

Tucker tossed the ball at his father and laughed.

"I know it doesn't change anything, or help in any way, but I talked to Sgt. Wilkens from the sheriff's investigation team. He told me the truck was definitely on the wrong side of the road and going too fast. The driver had been delivering gasoline throughout the county for twelve hours that day."

Sarah whispered so she wouldn't wake the baby, "I heard several people talking at the funeral about the oil company. One of them mentioned they always push their drivers too hard."

Douglas Dawson had no surviving parents or siblings. He lost his parents to cancer at an early age. Barbara Jackson had been the only child of Florence and her late husband. Glen Jackson worked for the railroad until he retired at the age of fifty-eight. Two years later he died of a stroke only six months after the birth of his first granddaughter, Beth. As a result, Florence was the closest blood relative of Beth and Caralyn.

Caralyn chose that moment to open her eyes and begin cooing as she smiled at Sarah.

"You are such an adorable little girl. Yes, you are." Sarah kissed her cheek and then held her close to her breast.

Tucker stopped running and sat on the couch next to his mother.

"Are we going to keep baby Tarry at our house now, Mommy?"

"She will be staying with us for the time being," Sarah whispered. "You can help me take care of her."

"She wears diapers. I won't change poopy diapers." He pinched his nose. "They stink."

Sarah grinned and said, "You won't have to help with that, but maybe you could help give her a bath."

"She can't play with my boat and turtle."

"She is too young to play with your toys, Tuck."

"Is she going to be my baby sister?"

"She won't be your sister, but she might stay with us every day. We will see what happens in the future," Mom told Tucker as she ruffled his brown hair.

He showed his ball to the baby, and then tossed it toward his father. "I can throw it even farther."

Sarah looked at Jim. He looked at her and removed his wire-rimmed glasses and pinched the bridge of his nose. They both thought about those words. The future. Had it not been for her headache that night, she and Jim would have been in the Dawson's car.

Chapter Two

"Mommy, can I take Carrie to the sandbox so we can play?" Tucker asked as he held onto the handle of a yellow plastic bucket with two red shovels inside.

"Okay, but you need to be careful and help her down the steps, Tuck. She likes to run all over the yard now."

"I'll keep an eye on her, and I won't let her eat any more sand. I promise!"

Tucker held Caralyn's hand as they climbed down the steps at the back of the utility room.

"Good job, Carrie. You climbed down backward and didn't fall," Tucker said.

They dashed to the sandbox located under a large maple tree next to the white two-car garage.

"Carrie, you can't eat the sand. We can build a castle and then knock it down. Won't that be fun?"

She jabbered at him and grabbed the shovel and started filling the bucket. More sand ended up out of the bucket than in it. Mom sat in a lawn chair, untied the red bandana holding her light brown hair in place and shook her head releasing her shoulder-length hair. She glanced at the kids as she snapped green beans from Grandma Stanfield's garden.

"Mom, look. We made a castle and Carrie helped," Tucker hollered as he stomped the sand castle into oblivion.

"It looked very nice. Can you build something else?"

"We can build... a... we can build a barn."

Caralyn ran in a jerky manner as fast as her short little legs could manage to where Mom sat and held up her arms.

"Me hold you," she said.

Mom grinned and set her large orange Tupperware bowl of beans on the ground. She picked Caralyn up and held her on her lap.

"Me wuv you, Mommy," Caralyn said as she put her arms around Sarah.

A year after the accident Sarah still took care of Caralyn during the day while Mrs. Jackson taught high school French in the nearby county seat of Butler. As Caralyn learned to talk she heard Tucker call his parents Mom and Dad, so quite naturally she called the McKays, Mom and Dad, too. She called Florence, Gam-maw. Despite the nearly three year difference in their ages, Tucker enjoyed playing with his "little sister."

"I'm home, Sarah," Florence said Friday afternoon. "I would have been home earlier, but I needed to talk to a student."

"It's okay. We don't mind taking care of Caralyn. She's taking a nap now. She and Tucker were chasing each other around the yard and it wore her out."

"She is a bundle of energy," Florence said. "I would lose twenty pounds if I had to chase her all day."

"You don't have five pounds to lose, Florence. You're as thin as a rail."

"I don't cook much since the accident."

"You could always come over for dinner."

"I appreciate it, but Beth is such a picky eater. Did she come home after school, or is she with her friends?"

"I saw her for a few minutes. She played with Caralyn briefly and told me she would be back after supper."

"Sometimes I don't see her until time for bed. I wish I knew what to do with her."

The Dawson home was sold and eventually abandoned by the absentee owner. It stood empty for several months then burned to the ground in the middle of the night. An investigation by the fire department revealed the cause to be faulty electrical wiring.

"Come on, Carrie. Mom said we could sit with Grandma and Grandpa." Five-year-old Tucker held her hand as they scooted to the other end of the hard wooden pew.

Caralyn gazed at the scenes depicted in the stained-glass windows of the Methodist church the McKays attended. She sat

12

next to Grandpa Stanfield, and he kept looking at her and smiling. She raised her arms and he pulled her onto his lap.

"Grandpa, you never held me like that," Tucker said.

"You didn't like to be held. You squirmed like a muddy piglet."

"Mom said we are coming out to the farm for dinner. Did Grandma make fried chicken?" Tucker asked.

"I believe she made chicken, mashed potatoes, and I think she baked an apple pie."

Tucker rubbed his belly. "That's my favorite and Carrie likes it too."

Caralyn usually joined the McKays on the Sunday afternoon trip to Sarah's parents' farm. She became as much a part of the family as all the other cousins, and Grandpa Stanfield spoiled her since she was the only female grandchild.

"That was good pie, wasn't it, Carrie?" Tucker said later as he and Caralyn chased each other in the fenced-in yard.

She nodded while holding onto her teddy bear and scampering after him.

"I'm going to the pond to do a little fishing," Grandpa Stanfield said as he grabbed his old bamboo pole from the porch that afternoon. "Who wants to go?"

Tucker shouted, "We do! Come on, Carrie. Let's go with Grandpa."

They followed him to the machine shed where he stored the large farm machinery.

"Can Carrie and me ride on the tractor with you?" Tucker asked.

"I suppose you can. You need to stand over there while I back it out."

They did as they were told and then Grandpa waved them over. He climbed down from the old Farmall tractor he still used to drive around the farm.

He lifted Caralyn into his arms. "Did Sarah change you?"

"She's got a fresh one on, Grandpa. Mom changed her. It was a poopy diaper."

13

Grandpa sniffed the new diaper. "You're good to go." He climbed onto the tractor seat and held Caralyn on his lap. She clutched her teddy bear and pretended it was sleeping. Tucker climbed up by himself and sat on the space next to Grandpa. He held on to the fender of the old red tractor.

"Hang on tight. We're going for a ride." Grandpa headed to the pond located past the pear orchard to the west of the big white barn.

He drove the tractor as slow as possible, but the ride thrilled Caralyn and Tucker. He helped Tucker jump down and then got down while holding Caralyn.

"Come on, Carrie. I'll race you to the pond."

Caralyn screamed and took off running. Tucker ran beside her and let her get to the edge of the pond first.

"I won, Bubby. I run faster than you," she said.

Tucker looked at Grandpa, and they smiled at each other.

"I know you let her win. You are a good... brother... to her. Shoot! Sometimes I forget you aren't even related."

"Come on, Carrie. Let's throw rocks in the pond." Tucker picked up a small pebble and threw it halfway across the pond. "Now you try." He handed her one, and she threw it, but it sailed backwards. "Try again." He gave her one more and she threw it. "Good job! It made it to the pond."

Grandpa smiled as he watched the kids. He remembered how his son Carlton would play with his younger sister, Sarah. He would let her win the race to the pond, too.

"Tucker, are you getting dressed? We need to leave in a few minutes," Mom asked as she helped Caralyn get dressed. It was the morning of August twenty-ninth. Tucker's first day of kindergarten.

"Me do, Mommy," Caralyn said as she tried to put her arm through the sleeve of the white dress with pink polka dots. "I can do it." After three tries she succeeded and smiled at Mom.

"You are such a big girl now, Caralyn," Mom said

Tucker came running out of the bedroom into the kitchen.

"I'm ready," he said with pride. "Carrie, I'm going to school today, but I'll be back later. What time will I get back?"

"We will pick you up at noon."

Mom helped Caralyn into the car while Tucker crawled in the other side. The ride to the school took five minutes, and Tucker jumped out of the car as soon as Mom stopped.

"Bye, Mom! Bye, Carrie!" he hollered as he saw his cousin Derren Stanfield.

"You get back here right now, Tucker James McKay," Mom scolded.

He marched over obediently.

"I need to give you a kiss."

"Aw, Mom. I don't need a kiss. I'm a big boy now." He was embarrassed because there were older kids watching. Neither one noticed Caralyn escape from the car and join them.

"I go school with Bubby," she said startling Mom.

"How did you unbuckled the car seat?"

"Sorry, Mom, I guess I didn't do it right," Tucker said.

Mom scooped up Caralyn in her arms. "Oh, baby, you can't go to school yet. You have to wait until you are older."

"No, me go school." She fought to get down. "Bubby!"

Tucker quickly walked to them as Mom struggled to hold Caralyn.

"Carrie, you can't come to school. I'll be home soon, and we can play in the backyard. Okay?"

Caralyn's lip quivered and tears poured down her cheek as she nodded. Tucker and Derren sprinted to the door where a teacher waited, but as he reached it, he turned back to Mom and Caralyn and waved before running inside.

When Tucker visited Derren, who lived in the country not far from Grandma and Grandpa, Caralyn would tag along.

"Carrie, come on. We're going to play Cowboys and Indians, and we're the cowboys. We will chase Derren and Davey. They're the Indians," Tucker told her as he carried his toy guns. "You can use this one."

15

She waved the plastic toy gun and shouted, "Pow! Pow!"

"You need to hold it like this, Carrie." Tucker showed her the correct way.

"Are we going to play in the woods?" she asked.

"Yes, we built a fort, and we are going to play there. Are you afraid of the woods?"

"No, I'm not afraid. I like playing in the woods."

Twenty acres of woods abutted the fifty acre farm where Uncle Carlton, Aunt Mary, Derren and his brother, David, lived. Caralyn learned to fish like the boys, and got into fights like them. She learned to stand up for herself and didn't let the older boys intimidate her.

"I'm starting school today, Tuck," Caralyn said. "Will you play with me?"

"Sorry, Carrie, but we can't play with kindergarten kids," Tucker answered. "But I will wave to you if I see you."

Mom walked Caralyn to her class. "After kindergarten is over, you will stay in my room. It's right down the hall. I have to teach second grade. Tucker and Derren are in my class, and you can play with them if we go outside in the afternoon."

"Do I have to take a nap?"

"You can if you want, but I won't force you," Mom answered.

"Is it okay if I read their books?" Caralyn asked. She put her hand to her face. "Sorry, Mommy. I forgot to use English."

Mom grinned and said, "It's all right. Grandma speaks French to you more than English."

Three weeks after school started the next year, Caralyn took several tests to determine her academic ability. She could read at a third grade level and her math skills were just as advanced. The teachers involved met with the principal and, after a lengthy discussion, decided to place her in Mrs. McKay's second grade class where her progress could be closely monitored.

Chapter Three

In December after Caralyn's eighth birthday, Mom and Dad McKay discussed an event from earlier in the day while in bed.

"Jim, I heard some of the older kids at school talking about... the accident. Do you think we, and Grandma, should sit down with Cara and tell her more about Barb and Doug?"

"Do you think she's ready to hear about them?"

"I'd rather we tell her before she hears it from the kids at school. I'm afraid they will make fun of her," Sarah said as she snuggled close to Jim. "I'll talk to Florence tomorrow, and see what she thinks.

The next evening after supper Grandma Florence and the McKays sat in the living room with Caralyn.

"Cara, we need to tell you about something that happened almost eight years ago."

"What is it?"

"Well... do you ever wonder why you and Tucker have different last names?"

"Not really," Caralyn shrugged. "Beth said it was because of an accident."

Sarah looked at Jim. Jim looked at Florence. Then they all looked at Caralyn.

"Beth said her parents got killed in an accident a long, long time ago."

"Honey, those people were your birth parents. You were still a baby when it happened."

Beth had known what happened, but she never divulged much about the accident or her birth parents to Caralyn.

"I'm not sure what 'birth parents' means," Caralyn said. "Can I ask one question?"

"What, sweetie?" Mom asked.

"Are you still going to be my Mommy and Daddy?"

Mrs. McKay hugged her. "Of course we are, sweetheart! We will always be your Mom and Dad."

"Good! I would miss you if you weren't."

She ran out to play with Tucker as if nothing had changed.

"Wow! That was easier than I thought," Sarah told Grandma. "Do you think she really understands?"

"Not really. She will understand better when she gets older."

"Do you think she knows Tucker is not her real brother?" Jim asked Sarah.

"I think she understands it, but I don't think it matters. They love each other anyway."

During her grade school years, Caralyn stayed overnight at the McKay house often enough to claim the top bunk of the hand-made set of bunk beds as her own. Shortly after Tucker entered sixth grade, Mom happened to notice Caralyn taking off her shirt to get ready for bed with Tucker in the room.

"Cara, honey, I know you love to stay in here with Tucker, but you are both getting older and... well... you need to stay in here by yourself."

"Why, Mommy?"

"Because when girls and boys get older they need to sleep in different rooms. And another thing, you shouldn't change into your pajamas when he is in the room." Mom didn't want to make a big deal about this, but knew she had to do something. "In the next few months you will take a special health class at school."

"Is that the one where the teacher talks about babies and where they really come from?"

"Yes, they will tell you. You may be a little young to understand everything, but you can always ask me questions if you would like."

"Okay, I will. I won't change clothes in front of him anymore because it kinda made me feel funny, and Tucker never changes clothes if I'm around. I understand that, but why does Tuck have to sleep on the couch?"

"You are getting older now, and you need a bedroom of your own. Just like at home."

Caralyn thought about her bedroom at Grandma's house. "But I don't want him to sleep on the couch. I want him to stay with me in case I get scared at night. I sleep by myself at home, and I don't like it."

"We are here with you at night."

"I know, Mommy, but if I get really scared at night, I get in bed with Bubby, and he protects me."

"Maybe you should get in bed with me instead of Tucker," Sarah said.

"Okay, but I don't get scared too much anymore. The other night when it stormed and there was a loud boom..." She moved her hands and arms in a big circle. "I got scared, and I wanted Bubby to protect me, but he was here and I was with Grandma. Why can't I always sleep here?"

"Grandma would miss you too much if you didn't sleep in your own room."

"Could I bring more of my stuffed animals over here. I have lots of them on my bed at Grandma's house."

"You can bring as many as you want," Sarah said giving Caralyn a hug.

"Did that bad storm scare you?" Caralyn asked.

"It startled me and made me jump."

Caralyn laughed and asked, "Did you fall out of bed?"

"No, but that was one of the worst storms I can remember. It knocked down several trees in town."

"Did anyone have an accident? Beth said a big storm caused the accident that killed her other parents."

"Yes, but not every storm is that severe. That loud and scary, I mean," Sarah explained.

"Good. I will try to be careful around Tucker, but he needs his own bed, too. Maybe we could build a wall right there." She pointed to the center of the room. "His bed could be on that side, and I can sleep on this side."

"We will figure something out, sweetie."

Chapter Four

Caralyn and Tucker rode their single speed red bicycles to the Lincoln Ridge cemetery on the west side of town. They raced to the entrance and jumped off their bikes, leaving them in the grass by the side of the gravel road. The summer wind blew harshly through the large maple trees surrounding three sides of the old cemetery. The sun hid behind a mass of gray clouds as a freight train passed. Its whistle made an eerie sound.

"That doesn't sound like a happy train, Tucker," Caralyn said.

"No, it sounds like a mournful train today. It's spooky being in the cemetery even during the day." Tucker watched the train until it was out of sight.

"Grandma told me my other parents are buried here. She said there is a marker with their names on it." Caralyn looked at the rows of graves. "Will you help me look for it?"

"Sure, did Grandma say where we need to look?"

"It's supposed to be at the far side by the train tracks. Will you hold my hand because I'm a little afraid of this place?"

"You shouldn't be scared. You're nine now."

"I'm nine and a half, and I won't be as long as you are with me, Tuck."

He took her hand as they began looking at the names on the headstones.

"Did you know any of these people?"

"There is a kid named Bailey in my class."

The trees shuddered as the wind increased in intensity. Caralyn squeezed Tucker's hand like a vise as they stealthily approached the last row of grave markers.

"It must be along here somewhere, Carrie." Tucker said as he listened to the trees groan.

They searched for a couple minutes until they found the headstone with the right names.

"This is it. Douglas and Barbara Dawson." Tucker pointed toward it as his fingers intertwined with hers.

"Grandma told me they were killed in a wreck when I was a baby. Have you heard that story?"

"Yeah, Mom told me she and Barbara Dawson were best friends and grew up together. My dad and your other dad went to college together. I think I kinda remember them, but I was still little when it happened."

They stood for a moment and gazed at the granite headstone. Tucker had his hands on her shoulders as he watched two hawks riding the warm air currents high above them.

"When a kid's parents die they're called orphans. I don't feel like an orphan," Caralyn said as she knelt down to pull a dandelion from the tall grass next to the grave marker. "I guess since I never knew them, I don't miss them. I know Beth remembers them, but she never talks about them. I know it's kinda weird that I call your parents, Mom and Dad, but that's how I think of them. Beth always called Grandma, Grandma, so that's what I learned to call her."

"I always call her Grandma, too. I know she's not my real grandma, but I still think of her that way."

"I know Grandma and Grandpa Stanfield, but what about your other grandparents? Where are they?" Caralyn stood up and faced Tucker. She shielded her eyes from the sun as it made an appearance.

"Dad told me his father died right before he started high school and Grandma McKay died when I was seven. She had cancer. I don't remember too much about her. She lived close to St. Louis, so we didn't get to see her very often."

"Did I ever see her, Tuck? I can't remember."

"You were still little, but you did go with us once or twice."

"At least we still have Grandma and Grandpa Stanfield," Caralyn replied as she looked at the other gravesites. "This is kinda spooky, Tucker."

"We can leave if you want."

"I'm ready to go. I'll race you to The Curve."

"Loser has to buy the ice cream cones," Tucker said though he knew she didn't carry any money with her.

21

They dashed to where their bikes lay in the grass. He let Caralyn reach the bikes first. She jumped on her bike and took off. As they left the cemetery, she looked over her shoulder toward the area where her birth parents were buried and waved goodbye.

In the fall Tucker started seventh grade in the two story, brown brick building, located only a block and a half west of the McKay home while Caralyn attended the grade school a mile to the east.

A year later when Caralyn started seventh grade, Tucker would wait outside Grandma's house so they could walk to school together.

"How was your trip to Chicago the other week? Did you do anything exciting?"

"Ray took me to a baseball game, and Beth told me more about sex. She told me about having a period."

"What does that mean exactly? Your period."

"Mrs. Heistand told us what it meant back in fifth grade when the girls had health class, but I didn't understand it all. I know it has something to do with babies and bleeding."

"Yuck! That sounds gross."

"I know! Maybe I won't do that because I don't want any babies until I'm really old, like Grandma." Caralyn didn't understand she wouldn't have a choice in the matter. "Beth bought me a bra, too."

"Why?" Tucker asked.

"She said I needed one because I'm ten."

Tucker grinned and said, "Ten and a half."

Caralyn rolled her eyes. "Only babies count half years."

Chapter Five

"Would you like a refill of your coffee, Florence?" Sarah offered. "There's more raspberry coffeecake, too."

"Thank you, Sarah, just half a cup, please."

A grave conversation about Caralyn took place in June shortly after her graduation from eighth grade. Florence, Sarah and Jim sat at the McKay's dining room table.

"Jim, you are the executor of her trust. I want to thank you for accepting that responsibility. I'm getting too old to know how to handle that much money." Grandma's hand shook as she held her coffee cup. "I know the oil company settled out of court to avoid bad publicity, but I didn't want to sue them."

"There was a lot of pressure on the oil company from their customers and the employees," Jim said. "Beth is showing much more maturity than I thought possible with her money. She is reinvesting it and living on a small allowance."

"I'm proud of how she finished college and has started a career." Grandma shook her head. "I don't approve of her living with her boyfriend, but that's another matter. We need to think about Cara's future."

"The years have flown by so fast. I can't believe she is already twelve," Sarah said as she heard Caralyn talking on the phone in the kitchen to her friend Nancy Young.

"That's just it! She's only twelve. How can she possibly be ready for high school?" Grandma Florence asked.

"It doesn't seem possible she will be starting high school already, but it's true. The fact is if we don't let her start and make her stay in eighth grade again, I'm afraid she will be bored and resentful toward us. She has always managed to adapt to the older kids without any trouble before. I think she will be okay," Sarah McKay expressed her opinion then looked at her husband.

He nodded in agreement. "As much as I don't like to see her put into social situations she might not be ready to handle, I think she needs to stay with the class she has been with for all these years."

"I know since I am her legal guardian, this is my decision to make, but I trust your judgment implicitly. I would rather not make such a difficult decision on my own," Florence said.

"You know we love Caralyn as much as if we were her birth parents." Sarah patted Florence's hand. "We would never want to see her put into a situation we didn't feel she could handle."

"I know, and she loves you the same way."

"Still, this is a difficult decision to make." Sarah took another piece of coffeecake just as Tucker walked in the front door. "Even though she would likely be the smartest student in the school. She understands the math concepts Jim teaches."

"Hey, Carrie! Are you going to try out for the cheerleader squad next year?" He grabbed a piece of coffeecake on his way to the kitchen. He stood in the doorway and grinned. "They need a midget to put on top of the pyramid, and I thought of you."

"Go away! I'm busy talking on the phone," she hollered. "And I'm not a midget, you cretin."

"Midget! Midget!" he teased.

"Tucker, leave Cara alone. She's busy talking to her friend," Mom scolded.

"But she is a midget compared to other high school kids."

After much discussion with the guidance counselors at school, and a long talk with Caralyn, Grandma Florence and the McKays decided to let Caralyn start high school on schedule. They would keep a close eye on her and try to protect her as much as possible. At least Tucker would be in the same part of the building now.

"I know where to go, Tucker. I've been in this building a thousand times. I won't get lost, and I'm not afraid of all the stairs. I've gone sliding down the rails before," Caralyn told Tucker on her first day of high school.

"Caralyn, you better not let anyone catch you doing that, or you will get a detention."

"I won't get caught, and you better not tell anyone."

"Just be careful."

"I won't fall."

"I gotta get to class. See you for lunch."

Tucker watched as she walked down the hall to her classroom. She looked out of place among the older, taller and more mature students, but that had been the case for several years.

After school Caralyn met Tucker by his locker, and they walked out the the east side doors together. They paused on the worn, stained, wide concrete steps for a moment.

"So you survived your first day, huh?" Tucker asked.

"Yeah, I talked to Coach Waters about playing basketball. She watched me play last year." Caralyn skipped down the steps.

"Are you gonna try out for the volleyball team?"

"Do you think I should? I've never played before."

"You'll catch on fast. You're a natural athlete," Tucker said.

"I'll race you home!" she shouted as she took off running as soon as they crossed the street in front of the high school.

Tucker shook his head. He waited a few seconds and chased after her. She looked over her shoulder to see if he was chasing her. A protruding edge of the sidewalk nearly tripped her, but she regained her balance and kept running. By the time they reached the porch on the front of the McKay home, Tucker was only a few feet behind her.

"I won! I beat you home." She gloated as she spun in a circle waving her arms in the air.

"I let you win, Carrie. I took it easy on you."

"Is that why you're breathing so hard? Admit it, I'm faster."

"If you want to believe that, then by all means, go ahead."

She stuck her tongue out and made a face as she opened the door and stepped into the living room. She let the wooden screen-door bang shut behind her as she hollered, "Mom! I'm home, and I beat Tucker in a race."

She casually tossed her backpack on the couch and headed to the kitchen.

"I heard you. How was your first day of high school, honey? Did the older kids cause you any trouble?" Mom looked up from the table where she had been sorting the mail.

"It was all right. Nothing real exciting happened. None of the older boys bothered me. They were all nice to me. I think Tucker and Derren made sure of it. I think the older girls will bother me more. One girl teased me about being too young for high school. She told me to go back to sixth grade where I belonged, but I gave her a dirty look and ignored her."

"Do you have any homework?"

"I finished it at school except for some extra reading for Mr. Green's English class. The math problems were child's play, and the French teacher doesn't know any conversational idioms. I wish the school offered Spanish instead."

"Superintendent Deschamps insists on keeping French in the curriculum because they settled the area, and he is obviously French."

"It's going to suck unless they change it," Caralyn said. "Oh, Mr. Green kinda scared me a little today."

"Why? What happened?"

Caralyn pulled out a chair and sat down. "Some of the boys were talking, and he yelled at them. I was concentrating on reading, and it startled me. He saw what happened, so he came over later and asked if I was all right and said he was sorry if he frightened me. He seemed very nice after that."

"I hope you like him, Cara, because he will be your teacher for four years."

"I think I will like him, Mom. He didn't seem so intimidating after he talked to me, and his class was interesting and not boring like the others."

"That's good, dear. Can you help me get supper ready?"

"Sure, Mom, just as soon as I run next door and change clothes."

Chapter Six

"Have you had any trouble interacting with the older students lately?" Grandma asked Caralyn in French at dinner one spring evening.

"Not lately. I found out there's one boy who's six years older than me. He has a beard and looks old enough to be a teacher."

"You've had an extremely busy year, Caralyn. You played volleyball and basketball..."

"I was a cheerleader for the boys' basketball team, too." She cut her pork chop and took a bite mixed with sauerkraut.

"Now you're playing softball." Grandma took a drink of water and added, "Don't you ever get tired. You've done every extra curricular activity except the school play. You never get home before five. You eat dinner with me when I'm home which isn't often."

"Grandma, I know you're spending a lot of time with Aunt Bernice. Is she getting worse?"

"Sometimes she forgets who I am."

"I don't mind if I eat with Mom and Dad sometimes. Tucker teases me, but I think he likes having me around."

"Does it feel strange to go back and forth?"

She shrugged and said, "I'm used to it."

One afternoon Mom sat on the back steps, sipped her peach-flavored tea and watched as Tucker, Derren, Davey and Caralyn played basketball on the hard-packed dirt court at the side of the garage.

"Shoot, Carrie!" Tucker hollered. "I'll get the rebound."

She faked a shot and stepped to the side. Derren slid to his right, and Caralyn slammed into him and fell to the ground.

Mom stood up and asked, "Cara, are you okay?"

She bounced up and smacked Derren's arm. "I'm fine."

Tucker ran into the house a few minutes later to grab the pitcher of lemonade Mom had fixed.

"Please try not to run over Cara," Mom said. "You are so much taller than her."

"Mom, we always look out for her."

"Remember she is a girl and not one of the boys, even if she wears jeans all the time."

"I know she's a girl, Mom. She is the cutest girl in school, but you better not tell her I said that, or she will get mad at me."

"What should Mom not tell me? Are you talking about me?" Caralyn had heard only part of the conversation as she walked into the kitchen, her face dripping with sweat and streaked with dirt. She ignored the bloody scrape on her knee as she took the rubberband out of her long blonde hair and shook it. She then bunched it up and fixed it into a ponytail again.

"Nothing, Caralyn. Mom was telling me to be careful of you when we play ball."

"I'm smart enough to stay out of your way, and I'm tougher than you think." She punched his arm.

Later that evening after finishing the supper dishes, Caralyn asked Tucker, "So you think I'm pretty, huh? I heard you tell Mom that."

Tucker snapped his dish towel at her butt. "You weren't suppose to hear that. I only said it because all the other girls in school are rather plain looking."

"Is that a fact? Does that mean you think Cathy Kingston is plain looking?"

"She's okay."

"Becky Jones?"

"They are seniors with college boyfriends."

"Are you ever going to ask a girl for a date?" Caralyn asked. "Some of the other sophomores are dating already."

"I'm too busy with sports to worry about stuff like that," he said. "I will have time for dating in college."

"Yeah, right." She smiled at Tucker, secretly happy he thought her pretty, but didn't let him know.

Toward the end of the school year, Caralyn had her first period. Since Mom had talked to her about the changes she would be experiencing, it didn't frighten her when it happened. She had been expecting it for several months.

She talked to Tucker about it a week later as they walked to school. "Do you remember a couple of years ago when I told you I would start having a period every month?"

"Yeah, I think so. Are you going to actually do that? I thought you didn't want to." Tucker glanced at her. "Do I really want to hear about this?"

"I found out, from Mom, it's not something where I have a choice." *You must not even know as much about sex as I do.* "I must be the last girl in my class to start. I thought I would never get it."

"Are you telling me it already happened?" Tucker asked.

"Yeah, two weeks ago." She looked up at his face and noticed the beginnings of a beard on his chin.

"Did you start bleeding? Did you get scared?" He grew concerned and backed up. "Are you still bleeding?"

"It happened during the night, so I didn't get scared, and it stopped last week."

"Was there a lot of blood? Did it hurt?"

"Yeah, and when it happens again I have to wear..."

"I don't think I want to hear anymore, Carrie." He told her as he waved to two friends getting off the bus.

"I promised I would tell you everything..."

"I know and I'm glad we can still talk about what happens to us, but I don't need to hear every detail. That female stuff is gross."

"I hope we never keep secrets from each other," Caralyn said.

"Okay, but maybe some things should be kept private. I'll see you after school. I gotta go."

Chapter Seven

One hot, muggy July afternoon the temperature hovered above ninety degrees with humidity as high. Jim McKay looked out the window and saw Grandma Florence. He rushed outside to talk to her. She stopped and turned off the lawn mower.

"Florence, no way you should be mowing the yard in this heat. Tucker will take care of it for you when he and Caralyn get back."

She removed her wide-brimmed hat. "I don't mind it, Jim. I need to get more exercise. I have been feeling a little worn-out lately, and the fresh air is good for me."

"You can get enough exercise by going for a walk later when it cools. Please, let Tucker finish the yard for you."

Grandma looked at what she needed to finish. "All right, but I hate to make him do it."

"It will only take a few minutes, and the heat doesn't bother him."

"I will give him a few dollars for doing it."

"You can try if you insist, but I bet he won't take it," he laughed.

Grandma Florence headed inside. Jim pushed the mower by the back porch. Later, Tucker finished the yard for her. He cleaned off the mower and pushed it into her garage. Grandma walked out her back door and down the steps holding a ten dollar bill.

"Here, Tucker, take this." She held out the money. "It's not much."

"Grandma, I can't take your money. I don't mind doing the yard."

"You should take it. You could take Caralyn to The Curve for ice cream."

He reached for the money, but withdrew his hand. "I can't. I've got money saved up from the other yards I mow in town. I'll use some of that to take her out for ice cream. Thanks for offering, and I will mow the yard the rest of the summer. No charge."

"Thank you, Tucker. You are a good son."

30

Grandma and Caralyn joined the McKays for dinner. Tucker took Caralyn out for ice cream later while Grandma talked to Sarah in the kitchen.

"I haven't been feeling up to par, Sarah. I don't know why."

"Have you been to the doctor for a checkup lately?" Mom McKay asked as Grandma handed her another plate to dry.

"I suppose I should see him."

"I'm going to make an appointment for you tomorrow. I will take you to get a checkup as soon as he can fit you in."

The next day Caralyn came over to help Mom clean the kitchen cabinets. They had been working for an hour when Mom decided they needed a break.

"Caralyn, before I forget would tell Grandma I made an appointment for tomorrow at two o'clock."

"Okay, I'll tell her as soon as I finish wiping out this cabinet." Caralyn stood on a chair to reach the top shelf. "I can reach it now."

"Oh, you know what, dear, never mind." Mrs. McKay waved a hand. "I'll go myself. I need to ask her about Mrs. MacCollister."

"All right. I'll keep working here." Caralyn sang an old Fridays At Five song as she continued to work.

Mom entered Grandma's house via the unlocked back door. "Florence, where are you? I need to ask you about the food we are going to take to Mrs. MacCollister. She's home from the hospital, but she still needs a bit of extra care."

Mom walked through the kitchen and saw Florence sitting in her favorite chair in the living room. Mom thought she might be asleep since she didn't answer. Mom touched Florence's shoulder and knew immediately Grandma Florence was not sleeping. She called 9-1-1 even though she knew it wouldn't matter. Mom slumped onto the couch and wiped her eyes. She thought about Caralyn. *Oh, my God! Cara would have found her if she hadn't been helping me clean. I can't let Caralyn come over here right now. I need to tell her first. This won't be easy.*

31

Mom fought back the tears, hurried back to the house and paused in the kitchen doorway.

Caralyn noticed the devastated expression on her face. "Mom, what's wrong?"

"Come here, baby. I need to tell you something." Mom told her what happened and held her in her arms while they both cried. She felt Caralyn's sobs as she rubbed her back and shoulders. "I know you feel bewildered right now and I understand."

Caralyn broke off the hug. "How did it happen? She was all right when I came over here. I never should have left her alone this morning."

"I don't think it would have mattered, baby. I can't tell for sure, but I think her heart gave out."

She cried for a while, but then told Mom, "I want to see her."

"You shouldn't."

"No! I need to see her."

Mom knew from her expression Caralyn would not be denied. She took her hand and together they walked across the backyard to see Grandma.

"She looks so peaceful, Mom. It's like she went to sleep and is never going to wake up." Caralyn brushed Grandma's hair and the side of her face.

The ambulance arrived, but they knew nothing could be done. The arrangements were made to take Grandma Florence to the Livingston Funeral Home across town. Mom and Caralyn stayed in the house while the paramedics took care of Grandma.

"We need to call, Daddy," Caralyn told Mom.

"I will do that right now, dear. We should call Beth after I get off the phone." Mom talked to Dad, then called Beth and told her the sad news. "Beth wants to talk to you, sweetie."

"Beth, she was okay when I left the house."

"It's not your fault, Caralyn. You can't blame yourself for what happened. Will you be okay, or should we drive down there right now?"

"Will you come tomorrow?"

"Yes, we will leave early tomorrow. Call me if you need to talk."

"We are ready to leave, Mrs. McKay," the funeral home director said.

"Thank you, Fred," she answered. "Cara, we should go home."

"Not yet." Caralyn shook her head. She watched as the paramedics wheeled the gurney out. "I'm ready now."

A few minutes later Tucker came home.

"I'm back! Where is everyone?" He walked into the kitchen, grabbed a banana and saw Caralyn and Mom talking in the living room. "Hey! Did I tell you about..."

Caralyn turned around at that moment.

He walked up to her, noticed her red eyes, looked at his mother and noticed she had been crying, too. "What's going on?" he asked slowly.

"Tuck, Grandma Florence is gone. Mom went to talk to her and found her in her chair. She looked like she fell asleep and never woke up."

"What? That can't be." He looked at his mother. "No way!"

She nodded. "I'm afraid it's true, son."

Tucker sank onto the couch, put his elbows on his knees, buried his face in his hands and sobbed. Caralyn sat next to him and held his head to her shoulder. Dad arrived home soon after and helped Mom start making phone calls. Soon the whole family knew and by the end of the day so did the whole town.

Beth and her boyfriend, Ray Gardner, arrived the next morning and she, with help from Mom and Dad McKay made the necessary arrangements. One of the toughest decisions they had to make was whether or not to allow an autopsy.

"It will help to know why," Caralyn said after learning what an autopsy entailed.

"It helps to know why something happened," Mom said.

The results proved the cause of death to be a heart attack brought about by arterial blockage.

Beth and Caralyn visited the nursing home to see Great Aunt Beatrice, Florence's older sister and the only surviving sibling, the next day. Beatrice was also Derren and Davey Stanfield's maternal grandmother. Beth explained what happened, but Beatrice didn't understand. Her dementia had gotten progressively worse, and she didn't always remember Florence. She had no clue who Caralyn and Beth might be.

During the next difficult days, Caralyn helped Beth and Mom McKay with the numerous details. They spent several hours looking through several boxes of old photographs Grandma had stored under her bed.

"Beth, have you ever seen these before?" Caralyn asked as she picked up another old photograph.

"I can't remember for sure, but I think I might have seen some of them a long time ago. I've seen pictures of our mother, but maybe not as a teenager. I really don't like looking at these old photos."

"Why not?" Caralyn asked as she looked at another one.

"They bring back memories I'd rather forget."

The night before the wake Mom McKay sat down with Caralyn to talk. "Are you all right, baby? I know how much of a shock this is for you, but you seem to be so strong about it."

"I have been crying at night, but I'm all right. After this is all over I will take time to grieve. But we have been so busy I don't have time to feel sorry for myself or anything. I am glad Grandma didn't suffer like Aunt Beatrice."

"Thank you for staying by me, Tuck," Caralyn whispered. "I don't know many people from Grandma's school."

"I don't either," Tucker said. "If you need a break, let me know. Mom said you don't have to stand here the whole time. Beth and Ray took a break earlier."

Another couple stopped to pay respects. They looked at Florence then walked up to Caralyn.

"You don't know me, but I taught with Florence. I'm Shirley Brubaker."

Caralyn grimaced as Shirley hugged her.

"I am so sorry for your loss, child. At least you have your sister for support."

"Thank you for coming, Mrs. Brubaker," Caralyn said. She looked at Tucker after the Brubakers moved on. "I am surprised so many people are here from out of town, and they all want to hug me and tell me how they know Grandma. Most of them are total strangers, but I recognize some teachers."

"I heard one of the teachers say how surprised she was you're a teenager," Tucker whispered.

Caralyn nudged him and replied, "Tell me. They must think I'm still a baby. One lady even asked if Beth was my mother. It's freaky."

The next couple repeated the routine and on and on...

When they were in a side room getting refreshments, Beth confessed to Caralyn, "I feel so guilty because I almost never came to see her. She would ask me to come, but I made excuses about being too busy with my own life that I never took the time. I would send her a card at Christmas but that was about all I ever did."

"I think she understood. She was really proud you made it through college."

"She wrote a letter and congratulated me," Beth said choosing a chocolate chip cookie. "It took longer than most people, but I did it."

Mom McKay kept a close eye on Caralyn—ready to be there if she needed anything. After the wake concluded, Mom and Caralyn looked at all the pretty floral arrangements.

"You did a good job choosing the songs for the service, dear."

"Thanks, Mom. She would sing those hymns at home."

Mom held her hand and remembered how only a few years ago she used to hold Caralyn's hand as they would walk to school.

Caralyn bravely delivered a short eulogy she had written without breaking into tears as Mom and Dad McKay beamed with pride.

"You did a great job, sweetie," Mom said as Caralyn sat beside her.

Dad McKay removed his glasses, dried his eyes and patted Caralyn's hand. "That was better than what the preacher said, honey."

Only when the casket was closed for the final time did Caralyn let the tears flow freely.

"It's okay to cry, Cara," Mom said when Caralyn buried her face in Mom's arms. Mom rubbed Caralyn's back and smoothed her hair. "You don't have to be brave and act like your heart isn't broken."

Caralyn held onto Mom's arm for the trip to the cemetery. Her efforts at being steady and stout had finally taken a toll, and she needed the comfort and strength only Mom could give.

After the service at the cemetery the family returned to the church for a dinner. Caralyn found the inner strength to talk, and even laugh at times, with her adopted family. Mom knew the hardest time for Caralyn was still to come.

Beth and Ray left right away for Chicago. Stockton Woods had no hold on them. With his long hair tied in a ponytail and earrings, Ray didn't fit into the conservative small town. Grandma had the foresight to know it would be difficult for Beth to handle the responsibilities, so the previous year she made Mr. McKay the executor of her estate.

Later that night after everyone had left the McKay home, Caralyn took Tucker by the hand. "Will you come with me, Tuck. I want to get some clothes from the house."

"Sure, Cara." He stood close and watched her pack enough clothes for several days.

"I don't want to stay here by myself. Can I sleep in your room?"

He started to tease her, but paused, then said softly, "You can have my room. I'll sleep on the couch."

Tucker slept on the couch, but shortly after midnight he heard Caralyn softly sobbing. He rushed in to hold her, and she cried for a time before she could fall back to sleep. Tucker got a sleeping bag from the closet and slept on the floor in case she woke up again.

When she woke up, Caralyn stepped on him.

"Ow!"

"Sorry, Tucker, I didn't know you were there."

"It's all right. You didn't break any bones."

She knelt beside him, kissed his cheek, and whispered softly, "Thank you for being here for me, Bubby,"

"Caralyn, we need to talk about the house," Dad McKay said two weeks later. "We know it belongs to you and Beth, but what are your feelings about it?"

"I can't stay there by myself, and I don't want to move to Chicago. Beth won't come back here," she answered.

"You are not moving, honey," Mom said giving her a hug. "You can use Tucker's room. He can keep sleeping on the couch."

Tucker raised his hand. "I have an idea. I'm tired of sleeping on the old couch. I could move into Grandma's house. I mean I could sleep there. I don't want to cook or stuff. I could even see if Derren wants to stay. It would be closer to school. How about it?"

Dad said, "The court may force Caralyn to live with Beth."

"No! I won't," she said holding back tears. "You are my family now. I won't move away."

Chapter Eight

"It's a good thing you don't wear make up or we would be late for school," Tucker said as he waited outside the bathroom for Caralyn one morning.

"Very funny, Tuck. I'm never going to wear makeup until I'm thirty years old. Go away and let me finish."

"Hurry up, or you'll walk alone."

She finished brushing her teeth and looked in the bathroom mirror.

"Did Dad tell you what the court decided?"

She smiled and bounced on her toes. "Yes! Mom and Dad are my legal guardians. I won't have to move to Chicago, but Beth said I can visit her every summer."

"Dad mentioned a document the Dawsons and he and Mom prepared before the accident. Whatever it was, the court thought it was important."

"Come on. I'm ready to go."

"That didn't take long. Of course that will change as you grow up. By the time you start going out with boys it will take you hours to get ready."

Caralyn gave Tucker a dirty look and stuck her tongue out at him. "I'm never going out with boys. They are too gross."

"You'll change your mind when you get older, Carrie. You won't always be a tomboy."

"Not if they're anything like you." She poked him in the ribs as she scooted past.

Caralyn, a thirteen-year-old sophomore now, wore her long wavy blonde hair in a ponytail almost without exception and fought if Mom forced her to wear a dress.

Playing on the sports teams and other school activities kept both Tucker and Caralyn busy. They sometimes bickered, as close friends do, but never got too upset with each other, or for a significantly long duration.

"I'm not a child anymore, Tuck. I can take care of myself. I don't need you to be watching out for me," Caralyn complained as they walked down the first floor hallway at school.

"Caralyn, I don't want you to get pestered by anyone. I know you're not a baby even if you sometimes act like one. Especially when you need something from Dad. You act like his little girl to get your way."

"I do not! You're just jealous because Daddy likes me better than you. Your own father likes me better."

Tucker looked at her, and she took off running—dodging the other students in her way.

She shouted over her shoulder, "You better not do what I think you are planning or else."

"How do you know what I am thinking?" Tucker quickly closed the gap between them.

"You are going to tickle me or something. I can see it in your eyes." Caralyn ran around a corner and straight into Mr. Green.

He put his hands on her shoulders to stop her. "Caralyn, where are you going in such a hurry? You aren't supposed to be running in the building."

"I'm sorry, Mr. Green. I'm trying to get away from Tucker because he is going to do something. He is probably going to tickle me."

At that moment Tucker flew around the corner and stopped behind Caralyn.

"Tucker, were you going to tickle Caralyn?" Mr. Green tried to keep a straight face.

"Of course not, Mr. Green. That would not be a proper thing to do in school," he answered with a straight face. "I'll wait until we get home."

Caralyn squealed, "You better behave, or I will tell Dad."

Mr. Green and Tucker laughed because they both knew Caralyn loved the attention she got from her best friend.

Chapter Nine

The McKays planned a party to celebrate Caralyn's fourteenth birthday. Mom sat next to her at the dining room table where she and Tucker were studying.

"Honey, would you do me a favor? Would you wear a dress for your birthday party?"

Caralyn looked at Mom and started to argue, but she decided to go along with her request. "If I agree to wear a dress, can we go to Butler and pick out a new one?"

"All right, since we have to run into town anyway I suppose we can look for a new dress."

"Thank you, Mommy." Caralyn smiled at Tucker who shook his head.

"You are the most spoiled brat in the world," he said.

The whole family traveled to Butler and planned to eat dinner after doing the shopping.

"I don't know why they make them so short." Mom shook her head as she held yet another dress up to Caralyn.

After searching for fifteen minutes, Mom McKay found a dress that met her approval. "Honey, how about this one? This is the perfect color for you, and you could wear it with that new sweater you got last month."

"Is it long enough?" Caralyn rolled her eyes. *Everyone is wearing shorts skirts and dresses this year. I don't mind showing my legs. If I have to wear a dress, it should at least be fashionable.*

She tried it on and it fit exactly right and looked perfect on her.

Mom said, "Caralyn, you look so pretty in that dress. It shows off your figure and you look more mature in a dress."

Dad and Tucker looked for new shirts, purchased several and rejoined Mom and Caralyn.

"Jim, what do you think of this dress?" Sarah asked.

"I like the color, but it's rather short." He pointed. "I can see her knees."

"Oh, Daddy!" Caralyn sighed. "I'm not wearing a dress that comes down to my ankles. Get with the times."

Tucker sat down and checked out the dress. "I hate to say it, but you look really good in a dress, Carrie."

"Tucker, will you please explain it's fashionable to wear shorter dresses now," Caralyn pleaded. *I know you like to look at girls' legs because I've caught you staring at Rachel Jardine at school.*

"I think you should wear what Mom chooses for you."

Caralyn stuck out her tongue. "You're a big help. Thanks for nothing."

On the day of the party Mom came into Caralyn's room, put her hands on Caralyn's shoulders and they stared at the mirror. "You look adorable in your new dress. Would you let me put a couple braids in your hair today? It will look better than a ponytail."

"Okay," Caralyn replied and then sat on her desk chair to allow Mom to work. "If I wear the dress to the party, can I change back to jeans later?"

"We will see," Mom said.

The McKays rented the grade school gym to hold the party. They even hired a local band. The Crestwood Tones. Caralyn invited all of her friends and classmates, and most of them showed up for the Saturday afternoon party. Mom McKay and three of her friends used the cafeteria ovens to make pizzas.

"Mrs. Young, you weren't obliged to bring a gift," Sarah said.

"I know, but I found this lovely top on sale, and I thought it would be perfect for little Caralyn."

Sarah took the gift and placed it on the table with a dozen other gifts. She looked at the teddy bear wrapping paper someone had used and chuckled. "Whoever brought that must think Caralyn is still a baby."

After the pizzas disappeared, Caralyn opened the gifts, totally stunned by the variety of presents she received.

41

"Mom, look at this paper. Isn't it adorable?"

Mom looked to see. "You like teddy bears, don't you?"

She opened another gift and held it up to show everyone. She heard ooohs and aaahs from the older guests. She whispered to Mom, "This is a kids size top. It won't fit me, but it looks pretty."

"Mrs. Young brought it, so please thank her. We can try to exchange it, but I'm not sure we can."

The band started playing and Caralyn walked up to Tucker. "I know you're nervous, but would you dance with me, please?"

"All right, but only because it's your birthday."

"Please try not to crush my toes, Tuck. I know you don't like to dance in front of people."

He had his arm around her waist as they moved in rhythm with each other, and only slightly off the beat of the music.

"I won't break if you hold me close," she whispered. "Come on! Smile and pretend you like it."

"Did you tell the band to play this slow song?" Tucker asked as he used his hand to wipe the sweat off his brow.

"Yes, don't you like it?"

"It's lasting forever."

"Just hang in there. It's almost over."

The band played popular cover songs, and Caralyn danced with several of her girl friends. The guys were shy about dancing. A few of the boys noticed Caralyn's dress, and Tucker overheard a couple guys mention her legs.

"Hey, Dennis, did I tell you she bent over in front of me to pick up a book in English the other day. She had on these tight jeans and ooh la la." He waved his hands. "Her butt looked so fine."

"You're an idiot. You do know that until a few days ago she was thirteen, right?" Nate poked Dennis in the side.

"So what! I'm only sixteen. In a couple years she will..."

"Shut up. Tucker is looking at us. If he heard you... well... you better hope he didn't."

Derren walked up to Tucker as they watched Caralyn, Nancy Young and Natalie Bledsoe dancing. He placed a hand on

Tucker's shoulder. "What are you thinking, Tuck? You look like you're in another place."

"I was thinking about Carrie and how pretty she looks today. I mean she really looks great. It's hard to believe she is growing up so fast. I still think of her as a little girl and a tomboy, I guess."

"Yeah, it feels like only yesterday she was playing Cowboys and Indians in the woods with her face covered with dirt. Digging up worms to go fishing, swimming in the lake and everything we did. Look at her now. She looks pretty good in that dress."

"Tell me about it. I heard some guys talking about her legs and her figure. I'm not sure I'm ready for her to start dating. The guys in this town are only interested in one thing, and it isn't basketball."

They watched Caralyn having fun with her friends. She saw them looking and waved. She thought. *I really liked it when you held me close, Tuck. It felt different in a way.*

The party wound down and everyone pitched in to help with the cleanup. Afterward, Mrs. McKay invited the family to the house for homemade ice cream.

"Mom, can I take off my dress now, please?" Caralyn stood by the kitchen counter and swiped the cake frosting with a finger. She stuck her finger in her mouth and licked it.

"Oh, honey! You look so nice. Would you please wear it?"

"Do I have to?"

"Grandma rarely gets to see you in a dress. I won't ask you to wear dresses all the time, but tonight I would like for you to do it as a favor for me."

"Okay, Mom. If it means that much to you, I will," Caralyn said with a sigh.

"You look so pretty and are beginning to look more and more like your mother at this age."

"Do I really? I don't think I look a lot like her in the pictures I've seen."

43

"Trust me, honey, you do. Especially your eyes and nose."
Caralyn closed her eyes as Mom McKay touched the tip of her
nose. "You aren't as tall and Barbara had darker hair, but you share
her facial features."

"I don't mean to hurt your feelings, Mom, because I love
you with all my heart, but sometimes I think about her and wonder
what she would be like."

"That's perfectly natural, honey, and I know you love me
and I love you, and most of the time I don't even remember I'm not
your birth mother. I think of you as my lovely daughter, I always
have. You will always be my darling daughter no matter what."

Caralyn gave Mom a hug and a kiss. "I will keep my dress
on for you tonight, Mommy. I love you and Dad so much."
Caralyn skipped away to find Tucker and Derren. She found them
on the front porch.

"Are you going to change clothes, Cara?" Tucker glanced
at her dress. "We want to take a walk around town so we don't get
stuck cranking ice cream."

"I wanted to, but I promised Mom I would keep the dress
on tonight."

Derren smiled at her. "You do look incredibly nice tonight,
Caralyn. I heard a lot of comments from guys at the party, and they
all were surprised at how nice you look and how pleasing a figure
you are getting."

She blushed and asked, "Are you trying to compliment me,
Derry, or are you just telling me I clean up nice?"

Derren shrugged. "Can't a guy compliment you on your
looks without you getting on his case."

"Thank you, Derry. It's good to know someone noticed."
She stared at Tucker and stuck out her tongue.

"Didn't I tell you how nice you look, Carrie? I thought I
did."

"If you did, I didn't hear you."

"I'm sorry. Caralyn, you look remarkably pretty in your
new dress, and I want to make sure you know it. Will you let me
give you a kiss?"

"No way, bucko! I don't want a kiss from any boy and especially not you," she said, but actually thought it might be fun to kiss him.

They shared a good laugh, and then Tucker and Derren smiled at Caralyn. "Come on, Derren. Let's give her a kiss."

"Stay away from me. You're going to tickle me, and I'm too old for that now."

She giggled and tried to get away as the boys moved closer and pretended to kiss her. Caralyn barged into the house. She scooted around the people in the living and dining rooms. Sidestepped through the crowded kitchen and into the utility room. She stood next to Dad McKay, who was cranking the old-fashioned ice cream freezer.

"Where are you running off to, Caralyn?"

"Protect me, Daddy! Those boys are trying to kiss me, and I don't want them to."

"What boys?" He adjusted the tub the freezer sat in.

"Those two!" She pointed at Tucker and Derren.

Dad laughed because he knew Caralyn enjoyed the teasing despite her protests. She sprinted out the back door and jumped down the steps in one move with the boys in hot pursuit. Caralyn sprinted next door to the front of Grandma's house and around the side toward the garage. Tucker and Derren split up to head her off at the back of the house. Caralyn looked back to see Tucker closing the gap and smashed straight into Derren's arms. He held her over his shoulder and waited for Tucker.

"What should we do with her, Tuck? Should we toss her into the lake?"

"Mom will be furious if you ruin my new dress."

"I don't want to ruin her new dress, Derren. I want to make sure she has to wear it all the time. She loves that."

"You know I hate dresses, and I'm only wearing it today as a favor to Mom. Now put me down and quit trying to look at my legs."

"We weren't looking at your legs, Cara. Derren was making sure your dress stayed in place."

45

Derren carried her onto the back porch of Grandma's house and deposited her on the swing. Tucker sat next to her as Derren stood against the white porch railing. She put her feet on Tucker's lap and leaned against the arm of the swing—just as happy as could be.

"Will you rub my feet for me later, Tuck? These new shoes hurt."

"What's it worth to you?"

"I will do dishes for you one night this week. How's that?"

"I suppose so as long as your feet don't smell too bad."

"Forget it." She kicked him. "My feet don't smell!"

Several minutes later Dad walked out the back door and called out, "Caralyn, Tucker, where are you guys? The ice cream is ready. Come and get it!"

"Be there in a minute, Dad," Tucker answered.

They got up and walked down the steps. Caralyn jumped onto Tucker's back. "Will you give me a ride please? My feet hurt too much to walk."

"All right. Hold on, wimp."

"I'm not a wimp! I can still beat you up." Caralyn smiled because she knew he would do anything she asked. She usually didn't take advantage of this, but sometimes she did and Tucker knew it.

"Hurry, Tuck! I'm starting to get cold," Caralyn complained.

"Do you think you can walk the rest of the way, Caralyn, or is it too far yet?"

"Carry me into the kitchen, please, or better yet the living room."

Tucker carried her into the living room and dumped her onto the empty couch.

"Thank you, Tuck. I love you." She smiled because she had gotten her way again.

"You are so spoiled, Carrie. I should toss you in the dump with all the garbage."

"Just try it," she warned.

"Caralyn, come and get your ice cream," Mom said from the kitchen doorway. "Since it is your birthday, you can go first. After we sing to you."

Everyone sang, even Tucker and Derren.

"Thank you," she said. "Can I have a bowl of peach ice cream, please, Daddy?"

Tucker looked at Derren and they shook their heads. "She is such a Daddy's girl. What will she be like when she grows up?"

"I'm afraid she will only get worse, Tuck."

Caralyn heard them and stuck out her tongue.

"Caralyn, that's not ladylike," Mom scolded.

"It's all right, Mom. We all know she's not a lady."

Caralyn waited for Derren and Tucker to get their ice cream, and they moved to her bedroom. She sat on the edge of the high bed with her feet not even reaching the floor. Derren grabbed the chair from her desk. Tucker sat on the desk after moving some books. The bunk beds of childhood had been replaced with a double bed when she moved into the house after Grandma passed away.

"Don't eat it too fast, Caralyn, or you will get a headache."

"I know how to eat ice cream. I wasn't born yesterday."

Not one minute later Caralyn made a face.

"Told you so," Tucker teased as she got a brain freeze.

"Shut up! I hate you guys."

A couple of minutes later she asked, "Would one of you kind gentlemen please get another bowl of this delicious ice cream for little ol' me." She batted her eyes as if she were Scarlet O'Hara from *Gone With The Wind*.

"Get your own." Tucker pointed toward the kitchen.

"Derry, would you be a dear and get your favorite cousin more ice cream, please?"

"Of course I will, Caralyn. It will be my pleasure. What kind do you want... Tucker?"

Caralyn tossed a pillow at Derren as the guys laughed at her. "I meant for me. I thought I was your favorite cousin since I'm your only girl cousin."

"Beth is my cousin, too."

"Shoot! I forgot about that."

"All right. I will get some for you, too, Caralyn. What flavor do you want this time?" Derren stood up.

"Banana, if there is any left."

Derren took their bowls and headed to the kitchen. He returned with a tray and fresh bowls of ice cream.

They had finished their second helpings when Mom came in to check on them.

"Did that fill you up? Do you want more?"

"We will wait until later and see what's left after everyone is gone," Tucker answered.

Mom collected the bowls and carried them back to the kitchen. Tucker looked at Derren and gave him a sly smile.

Caralyn twisted the end of her hair and asked, "Tuck, what are you planning?"

"Nothing. What makes you think I'm planning something?"

"I know that look and don't you dare. I'm wearing a dress."

"So!"

"You are supposed to treat me nice tonight. No tickling or anything."

"What makes you think I'm going to tickle you?"

"You were, weren't you?" Caralyn asked.

"Why should we? You told us earlier you were too old to be tickled."

Just then Mom walked back into the room. She heard what Tucker said. "Grandma and Grandpa are leaving. Come and say goodbye, kids. Tucker, be nice to her and remember she has a dress on tonight."

Caralyn jumped off the bed and ran to say good night to everyone who was leaving. Mom grimaced because Caralyn didn't pay any attention to her dress.

"Mom, is it all right if I stay with the guys tonight?" Caralyn asked after all the guests, except Darren, were gone. "Please? We won't stay up too late."

You haven't slept in Grandma's house since she had passed away. Mom thought about it for a moment. *I think it will be safe for you even with the two boys.* "You can if you want. Don't stay up all night though. You need to get some sleep."

"Yes, Mom. We won't be up all night unless she talks our heads off," Tucker said.

Caralyn grabbed a pair of pajamas, her coat and walked with the guys to the house. Memories of Grandma flooded her mind. She decided to let the boys choose where they would sleep. Neither one wanted to sleep in Grandma's bed so they came up with an alternative plan.

Derren told Caralyn, "I will sleep on the couch. You can sleep in Grandma's room."

Caralyn thought about it for a few seconds before answering, "I can't sleep in her bed either."

"That's okay, Carrie. I can understand why," Tucker said.

Caralyn thought of an option. "Why don't you guys use the bedroom, and I'll take the couch."

She looked at Derren to gauge his reaction.

"I don't mind the couch," he answered.

"You guys used to share a bed all the time when he stayed with you, Derry," Caralyn reminded him.

"That was different. We were kids then."

"Carrie, you can use your old bedroom and I will grab a sleeping bag and crash on the floor. It's only for a few hours. I'll be all right."

"I should go back to my bedroom, but I don't want to disturb Mom and Dad this late at night. They're probably asleep."

"Make up your mind," Tucker said.

"All right, I'll use the bedroom. I'm going to put my pajamas on now so I don't fall asleep in my dress."

"Good idea," Tucker said.

"Or should I keep my dress on so when I fall asleep you can undress me..."

"No! Please put your pajamas on so we don't have to go through that."

49

"Shut up! You're gross, and I hate you both." She marched out of the living room and into her old bedroom. She slammed the door and changed into her pajamas—a sweatshirt belonging to Tucker and a pair of gym shorts from school. She came back to the living room and sat on the couch.

"I believe that is my sweatshirt," Tucker said.

"Fine! Do you want me to take it off and give it back?"

"No!" Derren and Tucker both yelled at her.

"Gotcha! I'm never going to let any boy see me naked."

"Are you forgetting we saw you skinny dipping at the pond, Carrie?"

"You two don't count. I meant any other boy. And I was ten or eleven when we went skinny dipping."

"So we don't count as 'boys,' huh?"

"You know what I mean. Can we drop the subject and watch a movie?"

They watched movies until Caralyn fell asleep on the couch. Tucker carried her into her bedroom and tucked her into bed. He came back out with the sleeping bag.

Derren told him, "I thought you were going to sleep in the bedroom."

"No, I can't. She is too grown up, and I'm afraid something might happen."

"I meant on the bedroom floor," Derren said.

"Right. I knew that."

"Sure you did," Derren teased.

"Don't tell her, but she is so pretty and sometimes I forget she is almost my sister."

"Almost only counts in Horseshoes..."

"And hand grenades," Tucker finished the sentence.

"Sure you don't want the couch?" Derren asked.

"No, you can take the couch. I'll be fine."

Chapter Ten

Caralyn woke up early, stretched her arms above her head, yawned and then realized she was in her old bedroom. She remembered Tucker and Derren were here, too. She wrapped up in the blanket and walked out to the living room. She saw him on the floor in the large sleeping bag, so she lay next to him and watched him as he slept. *Tuck, you are starting to look pretty good. I like your beard. Soon you will need to shave every day.* She fell back to sleep.

Later, Derren woke up and noticed Caralyn on the sleeping bag next to Tucker. He was partially out of the bag and had an arm around her. Tucker woke up before Caralyn, and tried to slip away without waking her, but she woke up and looked at him.

She whispered so Derren wouldn't hear, "Did you sleep all right?"

"It was better than sharing a bed with you," he teased. "You hog all the covers."

She made a face and stuck out her tongue. "We can't sleep together because we might have sex. That happens when boys and girls sleep in the same bed."

"How do you know about sex? And exactly what do you know?" Tucker wondered if she could read his thoughts.

"I know how babies are made. Beth told me all about it."

"Oh, yeah! She did, huh?"

"Yes. In great detail. Babies are made when a man sticks his thing in... you know."

"No, we don't know. What thing do you mean? Where does the thing go? Tell us. Say it, Carrie."

"Shut up! Does it embarrass you that I know about sex, Tuck? I'm not a child anymore. I am fourteen."

Derren chuckled as he listened to their conversation. "Caralyn, you are still a baby in more ways than you care to admit. It's okay. We don't mind you are still a little bit of a child. You shouldn't want to grew up too fast. When you are older all the boys will be after you, and they will only want one thing."

51

"Whatever could that be, Mister Derry? I am an innocent young lady with no idea what you are talking about!"

"Cut the Scarlet routine, Carrie. You don't sound or look anything like her. Just because Beth told you stuff does not make you an expert."

"I bet I know more than you creeps."

Derren and Tucker shook their heads knowing this was an argument they couldn't win.

"Come on, let's get up. I bet Mom has breakfast made, and I'm starving."

They dressed and hurried next door where Mom indeed had breakfast started.

"You're just in time. Tucker, could you pull the cinnamon rolls out of the oven, please?" Mom asked. "Did you kids get any sleep or were you up all night?"

"I slept good, and we didn't stay up real late." Caralyn grabbed three plates from the cabinet.

"That's because you fell asleep before one o'clock, and I had to carry you to bed."

Caralyn ignored Tucker and got a plate of food. "Can I get something for you, Derren? You must be hungry."

"I can get my own, but thanks for the offer, Caralyn."

She ignored Tucker as a way of teasing him. She remembered how good it felt when he put his arm around her.

On a Sunday morning in early December Caralyn walked to Grandma's house to check on Tucker. She stood by the bed and watched him sleep for a moment and then touched his shoulder. He opened his eyes, saw her and then rolled onto his stomach.

"What are you doing here, Cara?"

"Are you going to Homecoming? Everybody in the junior class is supposed to participate."

"I know it, Caralyn. I don't need a reminder every day." He covered his head with a pillow.

"I keep reminding you because you are supposed to invite a girl. Have you asked anyone yet?"

"No, not exactly."

"What do you mean 'not exactly?' Either you have, or you haven't."

"All right, I haven't. Will you get off my back about it?"

Caralyn realized the whole thing bothered Tucker more than he admitted. She sat beside him on his bed and tried to console him. "I'm sorry about nagging you, Tuck. I didn't mean to. Do you have anyone in mind?"

"I thought about asking Cathy Thompson, but Darrell beat me to it."

"What about Brenda Lane or Diane Tate?"

"They already have dates."

Caralyn thought for a moment. "Derren is going with Natalie. Maybe you could ask somebody from her class or my class even."

Tucker looked at Caralyn and could tell she had a plan. "Okay? What are you thinking in that devious mind of yours? Spill it!"

"Well, I know Sandy Young doesn't have a date for Homecoming and neither does Nancy."

"Nancy is too young, and I don't think Sandy's dad will let her go, either."

"How do you know if you don't ask?"

"I know because Scott Robbins already asked Sandy, and she told him her Dad wouldn't let her go." Tucker pushed her off of the bed. "Go away. I want to sleep."

She yanked the covers down. "Mom wants you to get dressed and come to the house while they go grocery shopping."

Caralyn was determined to help Tucker find a date for Homecoming. Later that afternoon she lay on her bed reading a new novel by Jennifer Baran-Robbins and thought about a solution to the problem while Tucker sat at her desk and studied for a morning test. She closed the book and set it on her pillow. "I know someone who would be overjoyed to be your date, and her father would be a pushover."

Tucker looked at her with suspicion. Suddenly, he had an idea who she meant. "Carrie! Don't even think about it."

"What? I didn't tell you who yet."

"I know who you mean, and the answer is no way! I'm not taking you to Homecoming. I would rather stay home." He joined her on the bed and lay on his back.

"Why not?" She turned onto her side and used her elbow for support. "You aren't going to ask anyone else, I know it. You are going to stay home and be bored and feel sorry for yourself. Maybe I will tell Mom you are too afraid to ask a girl to Homecoming," she said and then giggled. "I'm going to tell them you are gay."

"You better shut up, Caralyn Ann or I will..."

"You'll what? I'm not scared of you. I'm going to tell Dad you are gay, and pretend I don't know what that means." She started to get off the bed, but Tucker grabbed her and pulled her back beside him.

"Caralyn, you wouldn't really lie like that, would you?"

"No, of course not. Beth told me what it means, and she has several gay friends. She told me how they perform sex."

"Did she really?" Tucker sat up. "What do they do?"

"I'm not telling. You can use your imagination. Now what about Homecoming?"

"You are a little blackmailer." Tucker looked into her eyes. "Fine! I'll take you but on one condition."

"What?" she asked with a grin.

"Do you promise you won't try to kiss me, or dance real close or anything?"

"Can I talk to you? Or is that forbidden, too?"

Tucker rolled over and climbed on top, straddled her waist and began to tickle her. She started laughing and tried to get away but couldn't.

"Tuck, stop it now! I'm going to pee my pants if you don't stop!"

"I don't care if you do." He kept tickling her, but stopped as she started to cry.

"Tucker McKay, stop please! I don't want to have an accident."

He stopped. "I'm sorry, Carrie."

She wiped her eyes. "I know you are. Are you still going to take me to Homecoming?"

Tucker grinned and said. "I will as long as you wear a diaper!"

"I'm going to hit you where it will really hurt if you don't get off of me this instant."

Tucker took Caralyn to Homecoming, and no one teased him about his 'date' for the night.

"Did you have a good time, Carrie?" Tucker asked as they walked home around midnight.

"I did. Thank you for dancing with me."

"No problem. I noticed you let several other boys dance with you," he teased.

She poked him in the ribs. "Darrell made me dance to a slow song. He even tried to kiss me and said he thought I looked pretty."

"He says that to a lot of girls, Carrie, but in this case he was right."

Caralyn slipped her arm around Tucker's and smiled.

Chapter Eleven

At the start of his senior year, Tucker got up the nerve to ask Sandy Young for a date. Caralyn found out and teased him as he tried to get ready.

"Why are you getting ready over here and not at Grandma's?" Caralyn asked as she stood in the bathroom door watching Tucker put on a tie.

"Because Mom took the shower curtain down to wash it."

"Do you want me to do that for you? You've tried four times to get it right."

"Yes, please."

She adjusted his tie and asked, "Are you going to kiss her? What if she doesn't want you to kiss her? Did you brush your teeth and put on your cologne?"

"Yes! Now will you leave me alone before I smack you."

"You better not, or I will tell."

"I should smack you for being such a pest."

"Go ahead and try, big boy. If you think you can," Caralyn hollered and darted to the bedroom.

Tucker chased her, grabbed her and tossed her on the bed.

She laughed at him. "That didn't hurt."

"I wasn't trying to hurt you, Carrie. I was only trying to get you to stop teasing me. I'm nervous enough as it is."

"Why on earth are you nervous?" She stood up, looked at his tie and straightened it again. "It's only a date with Sandy Young. It's not like you are getting married or something."

"I know, but I'm still nervous."

"You're still taking me to their house, aren't you? I'm spending the night with Nancy."

"Yes, I know. You told me enough times." He rolled his eyes. "Do I look all right?"

"You look okay, and you smell nice." She pointed a finger at him. "Sandy will tell us all about your date, so you better not do anything disgusting because Nancy and I will know about it."

"Trust me! I'm not going to do anything."

"Did you forget how?"

"What do you mean by that?"

"When was the last time you kissed a girl? Or held hands? Or anything?"

He turned his back to her. "None of your business, Caralyn."

"I bet you haven't even kissed a girl."

"I have so!" He frowned as he turned around.

"Who? Name one girl you've kissed. I bet you can't."

"You are going to get it, Carrie. Have you ever kissed a boy? I bet you haven't kissed anybody, either."

"That's beside the point. I am too young to be interested in boys yet. I'm only fourteen and Daddy won't let me go on a date until I'm sixteen. I'll be the only girl in my class who has never been on a date before I graduate."

"You'll be sixteen before you graduate."

"Just barely. Come on, let's get going. I want to see what Sandy is wearing. I'll be in the car. Don't take forever."

Tucker sneered at Caralyn as they walked to the Young's front door. He rang the doorbell and waited.

"You better behave, Carrie, or else," he warned.

Mr. Young answered the door. "Come on in. Make yourself at home, Tucker. Hello, Caralyn. Nancy's in the kitchen with her mom."

"Thanks, Mr. Young. See you later, Tuck. Have fun on your date." She blew kisses at him.

Sandy made her way downstairs a couple minutes later. "Bye, Daddy. We'll be back around eleven."

"Enjoy your evening. See you later."

Tucker opened the door of the family car for Sandy and they headed out.

"Where do you want to go, Sandy? Do you like Mexican food? We could try the Burrito Palace in Butler."

"That's fine with me. Are we still going to the movie?"

"We can if you want." *I've got forty dollars in my wallet.*

After eating at the Burrito Palace, Tucker drove to the drive-in.

"Have you seen *Rocky vs The Alien* already?" Sandy asked.

"Yeah, and it really sucked."

"I'm not interested in seeing it. Could we do something else?"

"Sure. We could go to the park and walk around," Tucker suggested. "I can handle that."

"Did we spend all your money already?" she asked.

"No, I still have plenty."

"A stroll in the park would be delightful."

Sandy talked about school as they walked and tried to get Tucker to open up.

Sandy stared into his eyes. *Are you going to try to kiss me? I hope you want to kiss me.*

Tucker kept looking at her but would look away if she looked at him. *Should I kiss her? If I do, she will tell Nancy, and Nancy will tell Cara, and I'll never hear the end of it. I'd like to kiss her, but will it be worth the trouble?*

They didn't kiss and headed back to her house. Mr. Young set his newspaper on his lap and looked at the clock as they entered and smiled. Nancy and Caralyn came downstairs. Caralyn pestered Tucker with questions about his date.

"If you don't stop, Carrie, I am going to take you home and make you stay there."

"All right, I'll be quiet."

They watched TV and then played Clue. When it was time for Tucker to leave, Nancy and Caralyn watched to see if he kissed Sandy.

Mrs. Young noticed and told them, "Nancy, give your sister some privacy. You and Caralyn run upstairs and get ready for bed. Right now! Move it, young ladies."

Nancy and Caralyn reluctantly headed upstairs.

"Do you think he will kiss her?" Nancy asked Caralyn.

"Probably not. He is too much of a chicken to kiss her on the first date."

Sandy came upstairs after a few minutes.

"Did he kiss you?" they both asked simultaneously.

Sandy sighed and said, "He kissed me on the cheek if you must know. You two are so immature."

Nancy and Caralyn giggled as they blew kisses at each other. Sandy shook her head and hurried to her own room.

Though Tucker and Sandy dated several times, the relationship didn't progress past the point of friendship. Tucker did take an interest in Nancy though. Nancy was two grades behind him, but she was eleven months older than Caralyn.

"Caralyn, would you give me an honest answer if I ask you something?" Tucker asked one day while they raked leaves in the side yard.

"Maybe, depends on what you ask."

"Aw, never mind."

She stopped raking. "You're serious, huh?"

"Well, yeah. It's kinda serious. Will you give me a straight answer?"

"Of course, Tuck. What is it?"

"Do you think Nancy Young would go out with me?"

Caralyn started raking again. "You know she would. She likes you. God only knows why, but she does."

"Thanks ever so much for the encouraging word," he said sarcastically.

"You know I'm only teasing, but Nancy isn't allowed to go on solo dates yet. She and I were talking about that the other day. Both our fathers want to lock us in a closet until we are old and gray."

"I agree with you, Caralyn."

"You do?" Caralyn dropped rake.

"I think you should be allowed to date now."

"That's sweet of you to be on my side for a change. Thank you. What's the catch?"

"No catch, Carrie. After all who would ever be crazy enough in this town to go out with you."

59

"You're going to get it. I knew you had some smart-ass comment to make."

"Caralyn, you better watch your language. Mom will wash your mouth out with soap if she hears you talking like that."

"Maybe you and Nancy could go on a date, if you agree to take me along."

"Why on earth would I do that? If I took you along, Nancy wouldn't even talk to me. She would spend the whole time talking to you. I would be lucky to ask her one thing. What if I wanted to kiss her? Would you watch and make faces at me?"

"No way! Why would I want to see Nancy tortured like that. Besides you would be too chicken to kiss her. You never did kiss Sandy properly."

"You are in big trouble, Cara." Tucker chased her around the yard. He caught her and they fell into a big pile of leaves. Tucker landed on top of her and grabbed her arms.

"Get off of me before I start yelling, you big ape."

Tucker burst out laughing. "So it would be like torture to kiss me, huh? I think I will do it." He teased her by putting his hand on her mouth and kissing the back of it.

She shoved his hand away. "Tucker, you better stop before someone sees us. They will think you are hurting me and call the sheriff. You don't want to be arrested, do you?"

"It would take the sheriff two days to get here, and by that time I will have buried your body where it will never be found."

"Very funny! Now let me up." She struggled to break his hold but couldn't.

"Not until you tell me you're sorry."

"Never! I'll tell Mom you were trying to feel me up, and you'll be grounded forever."

He let go. "There's nothing to touch, Caralyn."

"There is so." She took his hand and placed it on her breast.

He instantly moved his hand away. "Carrie, what are you doing! You shouldn't let any boy touch you there."

"What does it matter if I don't have breasts?"

"All right, you have tiny breasts at least."

60

"Are they too small?" She sat up. "Am I a freak?"

"You're only fourteen! They aren't supposed to be real big." He helped her stand up and brushed the leaves away.

She grinned and said, "Beth did."

"How do you know?"

"I saw pictures of her when she was fourteen. It said so on the back, and she looked like she was a lot older."

"She grew up faster than you, Carrie, that's all. She... matured quicker and developed an interested in boys at an early age."

"That's not all she developed." Caralyn held her hands in front of her chest. "She developed some big..."

"Caralyn, I'm gonna... never mind."

"How do you know she was interested in boys at fourteen?" Caralyn asked.

"I heard Grandma Florence and Mom talking about it once. I think you should stay a tomboy for as long as you want, Carrie. Boys will be interested in you soon enough. Don't rush it."

"Tuck, will you help me with something when I get a little older?"

"Depends. What are you talking about?"

"I want you to show me how to kiss and make out. I want to know about that before I start dating, so I'll know what to do, or what not to do."

"You better not do anything! You are too young to even be thinking about this stuff."

"I know about sex and stuff."

"Just because you know about sex doesn't mean you are old enough to do anything about it."

"I'm not saying I want to have sex with anyone, dummy." She poked him in the chest. "I want to know more about it, that's all. I can't ask my friends because I would feel too weird."

"You could ask Mom."

"She still thinks I'm a child. Don't tell me I'm too little, or I will clobber you."

"I wasn't going to say that. I can't talk about this now."

61

They continued working in the yard.

"Well, will you help me or not?"

"All right! I will answer your questions sometime, but what makes you think I know anymore than you?"

"I want you to do more than answer questions. I want you to show me how to do stuff."

"Are you crazy? Can we talk about this later, Cara. Like when you are about to be married or something."

She tossed a bunch of leaves at him. "Fine! I'll grow up never being kissed or knowing anything about sex at all until I'm a hundred years old."

"When you get to be a hundred, I will tell you anything you want to know, Caralyn."

She frowned. "You're a jerk, Tucker McKay!" *But I'll get my way somehow.*

"I know you won't allow Nancy to go on solo dates yet, Mr. Young, but would you let her if Caralyn is with us?" The armpits of Tucker's shirt were soaked with sweat as he talked to Nancy's father.

Mr. Young smiled at him. "That wouldn't be much of a date, Tucker. Nancy and Caralyn will spend the whole time talking with each other."

"Yeah, I know it." Tucker sighed in resignation.

Mr. Young chuckled as he imagined Tucker on a date with Nancy and Caralyn. "Tucker, you can take Nancy out any time you want, as long as Caralyn is with you."

"Thanks, Mr. Young, I think."

A week later Tucker took Nancy on a date. Caralyn asked Derren to meet them at the drive-in. They watched a double-bill. Two cult classics. *Attack Of The Killer Tomatoes* and *Little Shop Of Horrors*. After the movies Tucker drove to Reagan's Diner for burgers and pop. Reagan's had an old-fashioned jukebox stocked with classic rock and roll 45s. Caralyn borrowed several quarters from Tucker and picked out her favorite songs.

"Does it bother you guys I have to tag along on your dates?" Caralyn swayed to the music as she sipped on a Cherry Coke across from them in the stainless steel booth.

"I'd rather not have you along, but I don't mind Derren being here," Tucker said. "Mom ordered me to pay for whatever you eat. I could save money if you weren't here."

Nancy poked his arm. "That's not nice. I don't mind that you're along, Caralyn. It's more like hanging out as friends."

Tucker managed to give Nancy a kiss without being embarrassed even though Caralyn was watching.

Caralyn grinned. *About time you kissed her.* She turned to Derren and said, "Don't get any ideas, dweeb brain. You're not kissing me."

He pushed her away, and she nearly fell out of the booth. "You're my cousin, pipsqueak. I'd rather kiss a duck."

After dropping Nancy off, Caralyn asked Tucker, "Did you like kissing Nancy? Are you gonna try to kiss her again and make out with her?" She asked with a subtle undercurrent of jealousy.

"It was just a quick kiss, Carrie. It wasn't like a real boyfriend-girlfriend type kiss. Did Nancy say anything to you about it?"

"She said she hated it, and she's thinking about becoming a nun so she will never feel obliged to kiss another boy."

Caralyn jumped as he poked her in the side. They pulled into the gravel driveway and parked outside the garage.

"Did she really hate my kiss?"

"Are you a total blockhead? Can't you tell when I'm yanking your chain. She liked being kissed and wouldn't mind if you kiss her again."

"That's more like it." He pumped a fist and tried to high-five Caralyn.

She shook her head and ignored his high-five. "Tell her I said that, and I will murder you dead."

Chapter Twelve

Near the end of her junior year Caralyn and Tucker were studying at the dining room table when she tapped his arm.

"What?" he asked.

"Since we're alone in the house for a little while, I want you to keep that promise you made."

He closed his history book, tapped his pencil on the table and tilted his head. "What promise?"

"You promised you would show me how to kiss. I want to do it now."

"No way!" He shook his head and reopened his book.

"You have to! You promised."

"I can't kiss you." He looked at her and shuddered. "What if my friends found out?"

"Don't you think it would feel good to kiss me?"

"That's beside the point. It would be like kissing a sister."

She stood up and put her hands on her hips. "I am not your sister! Some people might think I am, but I'm not." She stomped a foot on the hardwood floor. "How can you think I'm your sister?"

He could tell she was serious about this. "All right, Carrie." He tossed his pencil away. "What do you want to know?"

"I want to learn how to kiss. I want you to kiss me."

"Wouldn't you rather let someone else teach you? Like one of the guys from school."

"God no! I don't want to kiss any of those guys, just you."

"My kissing experience is limited."

"You've kissed Nancy a few times. Now come on. You promised."

"This is gonna be a disaster," he groaned.

She took his hand and led him to her bedroom. They sat on the edge of the bed. She looked at Tucker. Although they had grown up as best friends, her feelings for him were changing.

"Okay, what do you want to do?"

"I want you to kiss me, Tucker."

He kissed her cheek like a thousand times before.

She smacked his arm. "Not like that. Kiss me on the mouth like you did with Nancy. Pretend I am your girlfriend, and you want to have sex with me. Use your words, dweeb brain."

He laughed. "All right. How about this? Oh, Carrie! I need to make love to you so much. I crave your body right now or I will surely perish."

She stared at him and then rolled her eyes. "Seriously! Is that all you got? Is that how you would try to seduce your girlfriend? Where did you get those lines? Baseball Digest?"

"Don't make fun of me, Carrie. You know I haven't gone out with many girls."

"Two girls to be exact. Sisters to be precise."

Tucker gave her a dirty look. He got up and left the room. Caralyn sat on the bed and didn't move. A minute later Tucker walked back into the room and closed the door with his foot. He sat next to her and planted a kiss on her lips.

"How was that?"

"Better, but you need more practice..."

"Forget it!"

"I'm sorry. Can we get back to the reason we are here. You don't have to be nervous. I won't bite."

They looked into each others eyes for a moment. Tucker tried not to picture Caralyn as a little girl. She was definitely not thinking of him as a child. Tucker leaned closer to Caralyn and she moved closer to him. They met in the middle and their mouths touched again for an instant.

"Do you call that a kiss? Our lips barely touched."

"It's not as easy as you think, Carrie."

They looked at each other and then tried again.

"Don't hit me with your nose, Tuck."

"Sorry, but you turned your head. Hold still."

"I am. You moved. Do it right."

They kissed again. This time their lips connected without bumping noses.

"I think we are getting the hang of it, Carrie. I like kissing you. It's a lot better than I thought it would be."

"Did you think it would be like kissing a frog?"

"Something like that!" he grinned.

Caralyn smacked his arm. "Try it again. You're still not doing it right."

They kept kissing until Mom knocked on the door.

Tucker jumped up as his mother walked in.

"Supper's ready."

"Mom, we didn't hear you come home," Tucker said.

"We got home several minutes ago." She looked at Caralyn. "Cara, you look all red. Are you all right, dear?" She touched Caralyn's forehead. "You feel warm. Should I take your temperature?"

"I'm fine, Mom. I feel a little flushed. Nothing serious."

Mom looked at Tucker. *You both look guilty. What were you doing? Were you planning a surprise party? I don't need a fancy birthday party."*

They ate supper and afterward sat on the back porch swing at Grandma Florence's house.

"I think I will like kissing boys when I get older."

"Remember, Carrie, kissing can lead to other things, and boys will not want to stop until they take everything."

"Are you going to tell me how babies are made? Get real, Tuck. I don't need a sex talk."

"Very funny, Carrie. Do you know how babies are made? Do you know anything about S-E-X?"

"What is that? I only know when married people want a baby it starts growing in the mommy's tummy until it gets too big and then it pops out her belly button."

"You are so funny sometimes, Carrie. You can make me laugh even when I am upset."

Caralyn cornered him two days later in the utility room as he was filling the dryer. "Tuck, I need you to show me a few things about making out. You promised you would."

"We kissed a few times. What else do you want to know?" He looked at one of his t-shirts and threw it back in the washer.

"I want to know how to make out. All we've done is a little kissing. We haven't touched each other or anything else."

"Are you really serious?" Tucker asked as he looked into her gray-blue eyes. "You must be insane."

"Yes, no, but let's go somewhere else. I don't want Mom to hear us, or see what we're doing."

"Fine." He continued loading the clothes.

"I'm serious! Let's go now."

"All right! Give me a second to get my chores done."

He finished, and they left. He turned on a side road before Grandpa and Grandma's farm.

"Okay, is this private enough, Cara?" He stopped on top of the hill by the old Martin one-room schoolhouse. "No one ever comes out here."

"Yes. First I want to know what it means to go to different bases."

"Where did you hear that old-fashioned term?"

"I heard Mrs. Calhoun talking to Mrs. Millhouse at school. They were talking about their daughters."

"First base is a single. Second base is a double."

"I'm not talking about baseball, you cretin."

Tucker explained what he thought the terms meant.

"Are you sure? I heard these girls talking about it at school, and they said going to third base meant you were naked and ready to have sex."

He shrugged and said, "I don't know. Maybe it has a different meaning for girls, Cara. I only know what I've heard in the locker room."

"Show me," Caralyn commanded.

"You want me to kiss you? We already tried that. You almost broke my nose."

"Did not, and I want you to make out with me like you would if I was your girlfriend."

"Fine, but don't complain if you don't like it."

They kissed, and at first it felt strange to be kissing in the car, but then, as they continued, it became more exciting.

67

"I'm so glad you are not my brother, Tuck. We couldn't do this if you were," Caralyn said as they paused to catch their breath.

"It still feels a little weird anyway, but you are a good kisser. I'm glad you aren't really my sister."

"I still love you, Tuck, just not like a brother like when we were kids. Do you remember how sad I was when I found out you weren't really my brother."

"I remember. You cried because you thought we weren't going to see each other anymore. You were afraid you could never think of me as 'Bubby' anymore."

"I'm glad you still let me call you that, Tuck, and I hope you always call me Carrie."

"Do you remember when Derren called you Carrie? You smacked him and told him I was the only one who could call you that."

"I remember."

They kissed again and he asked, "Have you been practicing with someone besides me?"

"No, I haven't kissed anyone else but you, Tuck, but I like to kiss you."

She took his hand and placed it on her breast. He immediately pulled it away.

"Don't you want to touch me, Tuck?"

"No way!"

She placed his hand on her breast again and at first he was afraid to do anything.

"It's okay, Tuck. You can touch me there. I don't mind. It kinda feels good."

"Caralyn, you shouldn't let anybody else touch you like this."

"I'm not planning on it. I won't let anyone else even kiss me."

He kept his hand lightly touching her breast as he kissed her again. "I think that's enough of a lesson for today."

"Did you get excited because you were touching me?"

"What do you mean?"

She looked at his jeans and grinned.

"Carrie!"

"Come on! I know what happens when you get excited."

He felt his face flush. "We are going home, and that's all the lessons you will ever get from me."

"Wait a minute, Tuck."

"What?"

"What are you thinking?" she asked.

"I was thinking about the day you went skinny dipping with me and Derren."

"I was ten and you guys had your underwear on."

She took his hand and placed it on her shorts between her legs. He jerked his hand away because he was embarrassed and scared by his reaction. She was more daring. She put her hand on his jeans. They kissed again and by accident their tongues met.

"Did you like it?"

"It was weird at first. Kinda like kissing a lizard, but now I like it a lot."

She smacked his arm. "I'm not a lizard, you blockhead!"

"Stop yelling at me, or else we're going home."

"Are you afraid to touch me, Tuck?" she asked softly.

"I'm not afraid, but I'm not sure I should."

"We are completely dressed. Nothing is going to happen."

"I know that, but will you promise me you won't let anyone else touch you there?"

"Where?" she asked.

He sighed and pointed. "Down there."

"I won't, Tuck. Will you promise me something?"

"Okay, what do you want me to do now?"

"When I get older, I want you to be the first to screw me."

"Carrie!" His head swiveled as he looked out both windows. "You shouldn't use that word. Don't ever let Mom or Dad hear you talk like that."

"All right I won't. Sorry."

"It's okay. I won't tell."

"Will you promise to be my first lover? Is that better?"

"No!" he said moving as far away as he could without getting out of the car. "Carrie, how can I promise something like that. Don't you want to wait until you are married."

"No! I don't want to wait until then. Who knows how old I will be then. Beth sure didn't wait long."

"You don't have to do everything she did."

"I want to at least know what it's like before I get too old to enjoy it. I don't want to be like Miss Hargrove from school. She is so old and has probably never had a date."

They both laughed nervously.

"Okay, I promise." Tucker didn't think Caralyn would hold him to his promise. He assumed she would find a boyfriend when she got older. The thought of Caralyn with a boyfriend bothered him though.

"We should get back home. I wish we were older, Tucker. I think I'm going to like sex because it feels so good to be touched like this. Beth told me she was hooked on sex after she first did it. Maybe I shouldn't say anything, but she had sex shortly after she turned fifteen. She didn't say who though." She paused and then looked at Tucker again. "I am serious about you being my first lover."

Tucker gulped as Caralyn looked serious.

"Are you gonna ask Nancy to get naked for you now?"

"Carrie! Her dad would kill me if he found out. I think about seeing her naked, but I'm not going to do anything with her."

"I've seen her naked before—in the showers after gym class. Do you want me to tell you what she looks like?"

"No! I don't want to hear about that."

"Okay, but she looks really good," she said with a grin.

He looked at Caralyn and wondered if she knew more about boys than he thought. They headed home. They didn't repeat the session in the car, but the next time Tucker took Nancy on a date, he kissed her with more confidence.

Chapter Thirteen

"You better come home to see me, Tucker," Caralyn ordered. "Just because you and Derry are big shot college guys doesn't mean squat. Why did Midwest Central allow you in?"

"Because I'm such a great athlete," Tucker teased.

"Hah! That's baloney. Try not to get lost on campus. It's bigger than high school." She rose to her feet and said, "There better not be girls living next to you."

"There are guys on either side and across the hall. We met one of them already. Richard Laderman. He and Derren met in class. He's cool."

"I gotta run. Nancy is coming over. Call me sometime because you will miss me otherwise."

"Yeah, just like a headache," he teased.

"You are such a blockhead."

Richard popped in to see Derren one afternoon before dinner. "So you guys are cousins, huh?"

"Yeah, but he's almost like a brother."

"How big is the town you're from?"

"A little over a thousand, if you count dogs and cats," Derren laughed. "I'll be ready to eat in a sec. Hang on."

Richard looked around the room. "They must paint all the rooms with this grayish paint." He noticed a picture on Tucker's desk. "Who's the girl in the picture with Tucker?"

"That's my cousin, Caralyn. She's a senior back home and that's Uncle Jim and Aunt Sarah."

"Is she really a senior? She looks younger."

"Yeah, but she's like the youngest kid in her class. She's only fifteen. Don't let Tucker know you think she's cute."

"Why not?" Richard kept looking at the photo. "She's definitely pretty for a kid."

"He's extremely protective of her. Ready to eat?"

"Yeah, let's go."

Two weeks later Derren said to Richard, "We're going home for the weekend since there isn't a home game. You want to go with us? I gotta get my laundry done, and it's cheaper to take it home. Besides Caralyn has been pestering Tuck to come home."

"Is there room for me?" Richard asked while checking out three coeds.

"There's plenty of room."

"Yeah, I'd like to go with you guys. It's kinda boring around here if there's no game," Richard said with a chuckle.

"How long does it take to get there?" Richard spread out in the backseat of Derren's car Friday afternoon.

"A little more than two hours if we don't shatter the speed limit. We could save a few minutes if we push harder."

"I've never lived in a small town before. I lived in London as a kid, and then we moved to Chicago. What is there to do in... what is the name of your town?"

"Stockton Woods. There's not much to do in town. We grew up playing sports and working on the farms. We like it better than a big city because everyone is friendly."

When they arrived in town, Tucker told Derren, "Let me out by the grocery store. I need to pick up some things, and I'll walk home. If you wanna tease Carrie, tell her I didn't want to come home to see her. If you dare."

Derren stopped long enough for Tucker to get out.

Richard chuckled as he looked at the three block long downtown. "It looks like a typical town except it's caught in the fifties." His head swiveled around. "There's actually a wooden sidewalk in front of that small building."

Derren noticed where Richard was looking. "That's the barber shop. It's the only building that survived the fire back in the twenties. They used brick when they rebuilt the downtown."

"All the buildings are jammed together like the row houses in parts of the city."

Derren and Richard headed to the house.

"Hello! Anybody home?" Derren called out as he knocked on the front door. He opened it and entered.

"Derren, is that you?" Caralyn ran and wrapped her arms around him. "It's about time you got here. You must tell me everything about college."

"From the moment we arrived, or what?"

"Start with the highlights, goof."

"Cara, this is Richard Laderman. He lives next to us, and he's from London originally, but now he lives in Chicago."

"Hello, Richard, It's a pleasure to meet you," Caralyn said as she let go of Derren. "Derry, did you forget to bring someone?"

He looked around, "No, I don't think so. Only the two of us. Why? Were you expecting someone else?"

"Derren, stop teasing me. Where is he?"

"Who are you talking about, Cara? Oh, are you wondering about Tucker?"

Caralyn gave Derren a dirty look while poking him in the chest. "You know I am. Now where is he?"

"I'm sorry, Cara, but he decided to stay at school and study because he didn't want to see you."

"You are such a lousy liar." She turned to face Richard. "I will assume you are innocent in this matter and won't hold it against you, but Derren is dead meat."

"All right, Cara. Don't shoot me," Derren said as he laughed. "He stopped in town at the store to pick something up, and will be here soon. Where is Aunt Sarah?"

"I'm in the kitchen, Derren. Come talk to me."

"Hello, Aunt Sarah. This is Richard."

"It's a pleasure to meet you, Richard. Welcome to our home. I heard Derren say you were from London."

He nodded. "That's where I was born, but I moved here at age thirteen."

Meanwhile Caralyn knelt on the couch as she watched out the front picture window. When she saw Tucker come around the house on the corner, she yelled, "Here he comes!" and sprinted out the door.

73

Derren laughed. "Come on, Richard, you gotta see this."

They hurried to the front window and watched as Caralyn raced to Tucker and jumped into his arms. He barely managed to set the bag down he carried before she nearly knocked him over.

"Derren tried to tell me you didn't come, but I knew better. I miss you so much. Tell me all about school."

"If you get down, I will tell you."

"Carry me, Bubby."

"Don't you think you are too big for a piggyback ride?"

"No! Please carry me."

Tucker carried her home as she asked him thousands of questions about school.

"What's in the bag? Did you get me something?" Caralyn asked as they got in the house.

He set her down in the living room. "Now why would I get you anything, Carrie?"

"Because you love me, and I'm your favorite person in the whole world. That's why."

"The flowers are for Mom." He kissed his mother and hugged her.

"Thank you, son."

"And this is for you, Carrie." He pulled out the book *We Were 'posed To Get Married* by her favorite author.

"How did you know I wanted this?"

"Because you remind me every time you talk to me. I had the store order it special and hold it till I got home."

"Thank you, Tuck." She gave him a big hug. "I'm gonna start reading it now," as she ran to her room.

"Just a minute, young lady. You need to help me with dinner," Mom hollered from the kitchen.

"All right, Mom. I'll be right there."

A few minutes later Dad got home from Dickinson College where he taught in the mathematics department. He saw Caralyn and gave her a kiss on top of her head. "How's my sweet princess doing?"

"Oh, Daddy!" Caralyn looked at Richard as she blushed. *Please don't treat me like a baby in front of Tuck's friend.*

"Hello, Dad! How was school this week?" Tucker asked.

"Not too bad. The students keep getting younger every year though. How about you? Have you been to class yet?"

"Not yet. I thought I would wait until November or maybe December to show up," Tucker joked.

"Derren, do you think you can make him attend class once in a while?" Dad laughed.

"I'll try, Uncle Jim. But he thinks he can get by because he is a basketball player on scholarship. Oh, this is Richard Laderman. He lives in the room next to us."

"Richard, it's good to meet you."

"It's a pleasure to meet you, Mr. McKay."

"Where are you from?"

"Chicago now, but I was born in London," Richard explained everything again.

"Honey, I'm home," he hollered to his wife.

"I'm in the kitchen," Mom responded.

Dad gave Mom a kiss and hug. "I haven't seen you all day and I miss you.

Caralyn informed everyone, "Dinner is ready. Everybody find a place to sit."

Everyone found a seat at the dining room table.

"How was your day? Did I already ask about that?" Dad smiled at Caralyn.

"All right, but Mr. Leach gave us homework for the weekend. He has no idea how busy we are on the weekend."

"I'm sure he doesn't have a clue about the life of a young teenage girl."

After they finished eating Caralyn asked, "Do you need my help with dishes tonight?"

"No, dear, I can handle them tonight. You can play with the boys. Maybe Jim will help me in the kitchen."

In the living room Richard asked Derren about Caralyn, "Why did Tucker call her Carrie and no one else did?"

"Oh, I should warn you." Derren looked over his shoulder to make sure Caralyn couldn't hear. "Don't call her Carrie. She won't let anyone but Tucker call her that."

"Why?"

"It goes back to when she was a baby, I think. Tuck had trouble saying Caralyn so he called her Carrie or Tarry. She gets upset with anyone who calls her Carrie now."

"Thanks for the warning. I'll try to remember," Richard said as he watched Tucker and Caralyn talking in the corner of the room. *She's even prettier than her picture. Young, but pretty.*

"Where are we going tonight?" Derren asked.

"There's a football game in Butler. Want to check it out and then get ice cream sundaes at The Curve?" Caralyn suggested. "Tucker will buy."

"Sounds good to me," Derren said.

Caralyn looked at the guys, and they agreed to the plan and got ready to head to Butler.

Richard asked, "What is 'The Curve'?"

Derren explained, "It's the ice cream and burger joint in town where the highway curves. Real original, huh?"

"Cara, aren't you going wear something warmer? It might get cool later," Tucker said. "I'm taking a jacket."

"I'm gonna grab a sweatshirt, and I'll be ready. Haven't you noticed anything different about me?"

"No, why?"

She touched her hair. "I got it trimmed and curled it. Don't you like it?"

Tucker and Derren shrugged.

"I think it looks particularly nice," Richard said.

"Thank you, Richard. That's sweet of you to say so. These two yahoos wouldn't compliment me if their life depended on it. Let's go before all the good seats are taken."

"We'll be back late so don't wait up," Tucker hollered.

"The house is open, son, and there are fresh sheets on the bed. Your mother figured you guys would stay there tonight. Keep an eye on Cara and be nice to her."

76

"I'm not a baby anymore. I don't need to be watched all the time," Caralyn insisted as she slipped the sweatshirt over her head.

"Yes, you do, Carrie," Tucker teased.

She stuck her tongue out at Tucker and Derren. "I think I will sit with Richard. He is treating me nicer than you two."

At the game Caralyn sat between Richard and Tucker. Three guys, who were sitting a couple rows in front of them, kept turning around to sneak quick peeks at Caralyn. Tucker kept tugging on her shorts to remind her.

"Carrie, will you be more careful. Those guys in front of us are always turning around to look at you."

"Duh! I've got shorts on. They can't see anything."

"At least keep your legs together."

"I know how to sit like a lady, Tucker McKay." She elbowed his ribs.

Later the action on the field got intense and the crowd jumped to their feet. As Caralyn sat back down, the guys turned around to look at her again. She stared at the guys. While Tucker and Derren weren't watching she made a crude gesture at the guys—she gave them the finger!

Richard saw everything, laughed and said under his breath, "Maybe she's not as pure and innocent as everyone thinks."

Tucker looked at Caralyn later and asked, "Are you cold? You're rubbing your arms and shivering."

"I'm fine," she said. "You don't need to worry about me."

"Don't be silly. Take my jacket." He put his jacket over her shoulders.

"Thanks, Bubby. I was freezing."

"You will owe me, pipsqueak."

She looked at Richard to see if he overheard their conversation, but he was watching the game.

After the football game they headed back to Stockton Woods and stopped by The Curve for burgers and ice cream. The guys were hungry, but Caralyn ordered a small fudge sundae.

77

"You guys are pigs. How can you be hungry already?"

"We haven't eaten for three hours. We're growing men, and we need to eat more than a skinny little runt like you!" Derren teased.

"I'll show you who's a skinny little runt."

"Carrie, remember to behave like a lady."

"You're lucky, Derren. If I didn't need to be a lady right now, you would get it."

They left The Curve and headed home.

"This is where Grandma Florence lived before she passed away, Richard. Nobody is living here right now."

"I'm sorry to hear about your Grandma, Caralyn."

"Thanks, we were really close, and I miss her a lot. You guys can stay here tonight. There's only two bedrooms, but the larger one has two beds now."

"Where are you gonna sleep?" Richard asked.

"In my room at home. Why?"

"No reason, I guess."

They started watching TV and talking about school.

"Tuck, did I tell you about the twins at school?"

"No, I don't think so, tell me."

"Well, when school started I met these two guys, Blake and Bruce. They're not identical twins, but fraternal so they don't look exactly alike, anyway. I met them and started talking to them, and I asked them how old they were and they said sixteen. I told them my age... by the way, I'm fifteen, Richard."

"So I've been told."

"They don't think I look that old, but I am. The twins thought I was a sophomore like them, Tuck. You should have seen their reaction when I told them the truth. They play basketball and are going to try out for the team. We need all the help we can get this year since you and Derren and the other guys are gone."

"Can you talk faster? I understood most of what you were saying there even though some of it was in French," Tucker said.

She hit Tucker with a throw pillow. "Creep! I'm not telling you another thing." She sat next to Tucker and pouted.

Around one o'clock Tucker noticed Caralyn had fallen asleep. "Derren, look. She's asleep. I thought she was being unusually quiet."

"Should we wake her up so she can go to bed? Get it? Wake her up so she can go to sleep."

Tucker made a face at Derren. "Is that supposed to be funny?"

"It was when we were younger."

"Right. I'll carry her into Grandma's room and put her in bed there. I'll sleep in here on the couch, and you guys can share the bedroom."

Tucker picked her up and her shorts slid up to show quite a bit of leg. Richard followed into the hallway as Tucker carried Caralyn into Grandma's room and deposited her on the bed. She didn't wake up.

Derren and Richard headed into the other bedroom. "We'll crash in here, I guess," Derren said.

Tucker entered and opened a drawer to find one of his large t-shirts.

Richard asked, "What's that for?"

"It's for Carrie. She won't want to sleep in her clothes."

"Oh, did she wake up?"

"Not yet. I'll leave it for her, I guess."

Tucker returned to Grandma's bedroom and rolled Caralyn onto her back.

She opened her eyes. "Did I fall asleep?"

"Yeah, you did. Here's a t-shirt if you want to change."

Caralyn sat up and raised her arms over her head. Tucker pulled the sweatshirt over her head.

"My t-shirt, too."

He helped her with it as he sat next to her on the bed. "Do you need help unhooking your bra or however you get it undone?"

She yawned and closed her eyes. "Yes, could you unhook it, and I'll take it from there."

He tried to get it unhooked but fumbled with the small hooks. "It's stuck. How do you get this thing off?"

She sighed and said, "You need to squeeze it together."

He tried again. "Okay, I got one of them undone. But your hair is jammed in this one. It might hurt." He yanked on her hair and pulled it free."

"Ow! Tuck, what are you doing?"

"I had to pull it free. I wasn't trying to hurt you." He struggled but unhooked the other one.

"I can tell you haven't had any practice with bras," she teased.

He stayed behind her as she removed it and slipped the t-shirt over her head. She yawned then fell back onto the bed and closed her eyes

"You must be really tired." He removed her shoes and socks and watched her breathing for a short time. "Good night, Carrie, sleep well." He turned off the light and left the room.

He rejoined the guys in the living room and plopped into one of the new recliners. Richard stared at Tucker but didn't say anything.

"What?" Tucker asked.

"What were you doing that took so long?" Richard asked.

"She needed help."

"With what?" Richard asked after Tucker didn't elaborate.

"Uh, she wanted me to unhook her bra."

Richard raised his eyebrows. "Really?"

"It got stuck and I had to... you know... figure it out."

Chapter Fourteen

Caralyn wandered into the living room and saw Tucker sleeping on the couch.

"Wake up, sleepyhead." She shook him, and he grabbed her and pulled her onto the couch. "Let me go, you creep."

"Did you sleep all right, Carrie?"

"Yeah, I did, but I don't remember going to bed at all."

Derren and Richard wandered into the living room looking rather sleepy and sat in the recliners.

"You fell asleep on the couch so I put you to bed."

"Did you undress me?"

"No, I let Derren and Richard do that," Tucker teased.

"Tucker James!" Caralyn screamed as she turned red.

"He is teasing you, Caralyn," Derren reassured her.

Caralyn suddenly realized something. "Did you take my bra off and look at me, Tuck?"

He shrugged. "I thought you would be uncomfortable if you left it on. You don't normally wear one to bed, do you?"

She wrapped her arms around her chest. "Why did you say that in front of Richard? Did you look at me?"

"Carrie! I didn't look at you like that! I mean I saw you, but I didn't look at you like I would a girl." As soon as the words were out of his mouth, he wished he could take them back.

"How did you look at me then? Like I was one of the guys who just happens to have breasts."

Richard listened as she snapped at Tucker. He thought about his sisters and what would happen if he tried to put them in bed and laughed.

"Would you rather have slept in your bra?"

"No, of course not. I don't care if you saw me."

"Just so you know, I was behind you when you took off your bra so I didn't look at you. You were barely awake enough to put on my t-shirt. I had to help you." Tucker pushed her onto the floor. "I need to get up and eat. I'm starving."

"Ow! That hurt. I'm telling Mom!" She punched his leg.

"Go ahead, and I'll tell her what you did at the pond."

"You better not! You promised you'd never tell anyone!"

"What did she do at the pond? And what pond anyway?" Richard asked Derren.

"She went skinny dipping at the pond, and we caught her with her pants down, so to speak."

Richard's head snapped to Caralyn who was struggling to stand up.

"Are you going to tell that old story to everyone?" She got up and stomped back to Grandma's room. She gathered her clothes and darted into the kitchen. She let the back door slam shut behind her as she dashed home to shower and get dressed for the day.

"Where is she going?" Richard asked." He thought about Caralyn and again wondered about her innocence. He thought it strange for her and Tucker to be so close.

"Home," Tucker answered. "Hey! Here's a box of stale donuts. Anyone want one?"

"I'll pass," Richard said.

Derren grabbed two.

They spent the remainder of Saturday morning relaxing at the house. In the afternoon they decided to drive to the farm to see Grandma and Grandpa Stanfield.

Tucker suggested, "I'll take my car and stop at your house. You can leave your car there and we can ride together from there to Grandma's."

"Thanks, Tuck. I need to fill up with gas at the house. You can fill up, too, if you want. Dad won't mind."

Uncle Carlton had a five-hundred gallon fuel tank at the farm. They used it for all the farm equipment and the cars.

"Come on, Richard. I'll give you a five second tour of Stockton Woods," Derren said.

"Mom, we're going out to the farm," Tucker informed her. "We'll probably eat dinner there. You know Grandma will insist."

"Have a good time. Will you take this casserole dish back for me, Cara?"

"Sure." Caralyn grabbed a pie tin that also belonged to Grandma.

Fifteen minutes later Derren pulled into the long gravel driveway and parked in back of his parents' house. Richard got out and glanced at the metal building to his right.

"Dad keeps his tractors in there and a lot of junk he won't part with," Derren explained.

They moseyed inside, but no one was home. He saw a note on the kitchen table and read it.

"They're at an auction in Slaytonville but will be back later. They knew I was coming home."

Richard stepped into a room next to the dining area and said, "Someone likes to read. I've never seen this many books outside of a library."

"Dad likes to collect old books," Derren explained.

A few minutes later Tucker and Caralyn arrived. Caralyn reached over and honked the horn.

"Really?" Tucker frowned.

"I wanted them to know we were here, doofus."

"Pipsqueak!" Tucker smiled as he poked her in the ribs.

Richard noticed Derren didn't bother to lock the door when they left. "That would never happen in Chicago."

"It's safer here," Derren explained as they got in the back seat. "It's about a mile to the farm."

Three minutes later Tucker turned off the tar and chip road and pulled up to a white gate. Derren hopped out and opened it so they could pull the car into the barn lot.

Caralyn jumped out and waved. "Hi, Grandma! Hi, Grandpa!"

They paused from working in the large, fenced-in garden and waved at Caralyn.

Caralyn rushed to the garden's wooden gate, opened the latch and sprinted to Grandma and Grandpa. She gave them both hugs and kisses. Grandpa's eyes lit up when he saw her. He still considered her his only female grandchild, and he had always spoiled her.

After introducing Richard and talking for a few minutes, Tucker asked, "Wanna go fishing, Richard? We'll show you where Caralyn likes to skinny dip."

She retaliated by poking him in the side. "Tucker, don't say anything in front of Grandma and Grandpa. You know they will get upset if they find out I was swimming in the pond, let alone swimming naked."

"I won't tell them, Carrie."

They walked to the pond but didn't bother to fish.

"Were you really skinny dipping, Caralyn? Or are they teasing?" Richard asked.

She skipped three flat rocks across the pond. "Yeah, they weren't supposed to be here, so I thought it was safe."

"When did this happen?" Richard asked.

"This last summer. They only saw my butt."

Derren told Richard, "We saw more than her butt. She doesn't believe us."

Richard's jaw dropped.

"I don't think it's a big deal, but Tuck and Derren are not going to let me forget about it. I used to come with them when they were fishing. I would bring a large beach towel and work on my tan. Sometimes I would take off my top but I was younger then. I didn't care if they saw me and they usually didn't notice."

"She didn't have much of anything to look at," Derren teased. "Then or now."

"You guys are so mean to me. Why did you tell Richard anyway?"

"To embarrass you," Derren said.

Tucker grinned as he told her, "You brought it up, Cara, so don't blame me or Derren."

"You guys are creepos."

After dinner at Grandma's, they dropped Derren at his parents' house and stayed for a few minutes.

"How are you feeling, Uncle Carlton?" Caralyn asked.

"I'm feeling better, pretty lady. Who is this guy with you?"

"This is Richard Laderman from school, Dad. Where's Mom?" Derren asked.

"She drove into Butler to get groceries."

Richard checked out a glass display case in the corner. "My mother collects this stuff, too, but her collection is smaller."

"We need to get home, Uncle Carlton. Say hi to Aunt Mary for me." Tucker waved as he walked out.

"Thanks for the ride, Tuck. I'll be ready whenever you want to head back to school."

"You're driving. You tell me what time you want to leave."

Caralyn gave Uncle Carlton a kiss goodbye.

"Come on, Cara, unless you want to walk home," Tuck said. "Richard and I are leaving."

"Hang on a second, dweeb brain. I'm coming."

Tucker and Richard watched TV at Grandma Florence's house while Caralyn helped Mom McKay fold laundry next door.

"Can I stay at Grandma's house again tonight?" Caralyn asked.

"Okay, but don't stay up too late. Tomorrow is Sunday, remember?"

"Thanks, Mom. Night, Daddy, I'm staying with the guys tonight." Caralyn grabbed her pajamas and ran out the door to Grandma's house. "Mom said I could stay here tonight."

"Caralyn, can I see you in the kitchen for a minute?" Tucker asked.

She followed him into the kitchen. "What's wrong?"

"Nothing's wrong. I wanted to remind you Richard is here and you need to act like a lady. What pajamas you were planning to wear?"

"Good grief! I'm not going to wear anything he can see through. Are these all right?" She showed Tucker a purple t-shirt and a pair of gym shorts.

"Carrie, I was only looking out for you."

"I'm not a child. You don't have to take care of me."

Soon after finishing their Sunday dinner, the guys had to head back to school.

"Have a safe trip back, son," Dad said. "It was nice to meet you, Richard. Try to convince Tucker to check out a class once in a while."

Caralyn followed the guys to the car. "Can I come up and see you soon, Tuck? I want to go to a football game."

"We have a home game in two weeks. You can take the train, and I'll pick you up."

"Okay. Bye, Richard. It was a pleasure to meet you."

"I enjoyed meeting you too, Caralyn. I look forward to seeing you again," he said rather formally. *It would be good to see you away from your parents and Tucker.*

Caralyn hugged Tucker and Derren and almost hugged Richard. *I'm not sure how you would react to me hugging you. You might take it the wrong way. I may only be fifteen, but I can tell you think of me differently than Tuck and Derren.*

On the way back to school, Richard thought about Caralyn. *I wish she was a bit older because she certainly is pretty. God! She went skinny dipping in front of the guys. She's only fifteen and she can be so sexy. Her legs are so fine and the rest of her... Well, she is going to be a real fox in a couple of years.*

Chapter Fifteen

Two weeks later Caralyn caught the train to New Lebanon. Tucker met her at the station and brought her to Crawford Hall where he, Derren and Richard lived.

"Where are you gonna sleep, Carrie? My bed's not really big enough for both of us."

"Well, if you aren't going to share your bed with me, maybe Richard will let me sleep with him," Caralyn told Tucker and Derren knowing full well they would never allow such an arrangement.

"Fine! You can use the bed, and I will crash on the floor," Tucker said.

Caralyn changed into her pajamas and they talked until she could barely keep her eyes open. Tucker pulled his sleeping out of the closet and started to unzip it, but Caralyn pulled him onto the bed.

"There will be enough room, Tuck. I'll scoot next to the wall and won't take up much room at all. See! There is enough room for both of us. Just don't squash me."

Tucker and Derren woke up early and slipped out for a run. They got back as Caralyn did her morning stretching.

"Where did you go, Tuck?"

"We ducked out for a run. Are you hungry?"

"Yeah! Can we go out for breakfast? I have a taste for restaurant pancakes. Can we ask Richard?"

"Sure, I'll join you," he said later. "When did you get here, Caralyn?"

"I came up on the train and stayed with Tuck and Derren last night."

Richard looked at her quizzically. "Where did you sleep?"

"In Tucker's bed," she answered matter-of-factly.

He cocked his head. "Really? Get serious."

"There was barely enough room for both of us. He didn't squash me, but he did get almost on top of me."

"I ended up on the floor in a sleeping bag," Tucker said. "I waited until she fell asleep before I moved."

Richard looked at her, but didn't say anything more about the sleeping arrangements. After breakfast they had time to kill.

"It's a lot cooler than when you guys came home a couple of weeks ago," Caralyn mentioned to Tucker and Derren.

"It is that time of year, Carrie," Tucker teased.

Tucker and Richard took her on a short tour of the campus while Derren caught up on his studying. Richard fell a few steps behind them as he intentionally slowed. *You have a cute little butt. Shoot! I have to remember you're only fifteen and Tucker's little sister.* He stopped walking for a moment. *Derren is sure right. Tucker is awfully protective of her and she adores him.*

They headed to the stadium at eleven to catch the game. Caralyn sat between Tucker and Richard with Derren at the end of the aisle. When MCU scored, she high-fived Tucker with both hands and then turned to Richard with her hands still in the air. She caught him looking at her chest and grinned.

"What does everyone want for supper?" Caralyn asked after the game, "Is there a place close by to get good pizza?"

"We could check out Antonio's Pizza Palace if you want, Carrie. Would that be all right?"

"Okay with me. Is that okay with you, Derry?"

"Wherever you want, Cara. We should go early before it gets too crowded."

"Are you coming, too, Richard?" Caralyn asked. "Tucker will pay. He has to pay for me. Dad said so."

"If you don't mind me tagging along, I'll join you."

She grabbed his arm, smiled and told him, "I don't mind if you come along."

Richard smiled back and whispered, "You are quite the little flirt, young lady. I like that."

After hanging out at the pizza place, they walked around campus for an hour.

"My roommate isn't here. There is an empty bed. Caralyn could stay there so she doesn't have to sleep with Tucker."

They looked at him with open mouths.

"I didn't mean it like that, you guys. I merely thought since there is an empty bed, it would be more comfortable than you sleeping with Caralyn. There can't be much room for both of you."

"There was enough room in your bed when you had that girl from down the hall spend the night with you last week," Tucker said.

Caralyn looked at Tucker and then at Richard. "You spent the night with a girl?"

"We aren't a couple or anything," Richard said. "Didn't mean anything."

Caralyn looked at him with dismay and a trace of disappointment in her voice. "So it was just a night of casual sex then, huh?"

"I was completely serious about it," he whispered. "Do I detect some jealousy?"

"No!" she said angrily.

"Maybe I could stay with Richard, and Cara could use my bed," Derren offered. "Tucker can use a bed instead of the floor."

"Yeah, that would be fine," Richard nodded. "I didn't mean to give you the impression I wanted to sleep with you, Caralyn." *Crap! I better shut up before I make this any worse.*

"Richard! Don't you think I'm a little too young to even be thinking of things like that." Caralyn shot him down with a frown.

"Sorry, I know you are still too young to be, oh, never mind. I'm sorry I brought it up the way I did. It would be better if Derren slept in the empty bed."

Caralyn looked at Richard, and wondered, *How many girls have you slept with? Would you try to get me in your bed even if you are friends with Tucker and Derren?* She shifted her gaze to Tucker. *You better not be doing that, or I will murder you severely.*

They returned to Tucker and Derren's room. Caralyn sat on Tucker's bed against the wall and Tucker rested his head in her lap.

Later, a girl stopped by to see Richard. Caralyn frowned at him as he left.

"If that girl stays with Richard, where will you sleep, Derry?" Caralyn asked.

"I might crash with a friend. It's okay," he answered.

"Does Richard do that all the time? Why doesn't he find a girl he really likes and stick with her?" Caralyn asked.

"Not sure, but he will figure it out," Tucker answered.

"He better before he ends up with a disease."

The next morning the four of them joined other kids for a game of two-hand-touch football. Caralyn joined Tucker and Derren on one team, but Richard played on the other side. A couple of times Richard had to stop Caralyn after she caught passes. One time his hand slipped as she sprinted past.

Caralyn smiled at him as they walked back to their huddles. "Richard! Were you trying to grab my butt?"

"No! Why would you... never mind." His face reddened. "I didn't mean to touch you there."

She giggled and wiggled her butt at him before going back to the huddle.

"Carrie, quit flirting with him," Tucker scolded.

"I'm teasing him because I'm better at football."

A few plays later Richard got blocked by one of the players and fell on top of Caralyn.

"I'm sorry!" he exclaimed as he looked into her face. He felt thoroughly embarrassed because her face expressed shock.

Gradually, a smile started to appear. He looked at her lips and for a brief second he thought about kissing her.

Caralyn lay on her back and stared into Richard's eyes. "Are you going to help me up anytime soon?"

Richard helped her up. "Sorry, I was... never mind."

"Are you okay, Carrie?" Tucker asked.

"I'm fine, but what happened. One second I was standing there and the next thing I knew Richard hit me and we fell to the ground."

"He got blocked into you, Cara. It wasn't his fault," Derren told her.

"I'm hungry. Is anyone else ready for lunch?" Caralyn asked as she jumped on Tucker's back after the game.

"What do you have a taste for, Cara?" Derren asked.

"Is there a good place for Mexican around here?"

"Yeah, there is a place called El Burrito Rico a few blocks away. It's real good, and it's usually not crowded on Sundays."

"Sounds good to me." Caralyn jumped down from Tucker's back. "Are you mad because I'm a better football player than you?" Caralyn teased Richard as they walked to the restaurant.

"I could beat you at tennis." Richard hit a forehand shot with an imaginary racquet. "I played on my high school team."

They placed their order and as Derren and Tucker waited at the counter for the food, they heard Caralyn giggling. She and Richard kept bumping hips as they filled four cups with either root beer or Dr Pepper. They carried the pop to a corner booth and sat on the same side while Tucker and Derren waited at the counter for their food.

"You felt me up when you landed on me," she said.

"It was an accident," he insisted.

"Maybe at first, but you kept your hand there longer than you needed."

"Then I apologize."

"Apology accepted," she said and then grinned. "You thought about kissing me, didn't you?"

"Have you ever tried beer or wine, Caralyn?" Richard asked to change the subject.

"Of course not! Why? Have you?"

"Sure. We always had it around the house, and my parents didn't care if I drank it occasionally."

"Have you ever been drunk?" Caralyn asked after taking a drink of her root beer.

"Not really. One time I had maybe one too many, but I didn't get drunk. When you get older are you going to try beer at least? Tucker and Derren won't even try it."

91

"I might. I tried it once and didn't like the smell, but I won't be afraid to at least try it again. I almost had some once, but … never mind. It's a long story. Don't tell Derren or Tuck I said that. Tucker would be pissed if he knew I was drinking beer." She leaned closer and asked, "Did you have sex with the girl I saw?"

Richard almost choked as he swallowed his Dr Pepper the wrong way. "No, I stayed in her room to study."

"You're a creep. Would you offer me some beer and try to get me drunk so you could have your way with me?"

He laughed. "Maybe I would. You can never tell."

Caralyn knew Richard was really flirting with her now. The guys arrived with the food.

"What were you guys doing at the fountain?" Tucker asked. "I could hear you giggling."

"He kept bumping his hip against me trying to make me spill the pop. Which one of these bottles is the hot stuff? I want to put some on my rice and beans."

"The green stuff is milder, Carrie."

She looked at Tucker trying to decide if he was lying.

"Derry, is he telling the truth?"

"Yes, the red sauce is actually hotter."

Richard grabbed the bottle of red sauce and squirted a generous amount on his food.

"I want to try a little bit of the red sauce."

She squeezed a tiny bit on her rice and tried it. "That's not real hot." Within thirty seconds her eyes and nose betrayed her.

Tucker and Derren laughed as she suffered.

"All right. I admit it's too hot for me." She kicked Tucker's shin and stuck out her tongue.

Three o'clock arrived, and Caralyn needed to catch the train home. Tucker and Richard took her to the station.

"Thanks for letting me stay with you and paying for everything. I didn't spend any of the money Dad gave me."

"It was fun with you here, Caralyn. Come back soon." Richard tried not to sound like he was flirting.

Tucker put his hand on her shoulder. "Let me know when you want to come back. There are still football games left and you can come to some basketball games."

She gave Richard a hug goodbye. Then she hugged Tucker, and he kissed her cheek.

Tucker and Richard watched as the train pulled away. Caralyn waved goodbye and blew kisses through the window.

"You and Caralyn are unusually close, aren't you?" Richard asked as they walked back to the car.

"Yeah, we are. We are best friends, and it's hard to be away from her, but next year she will be here at school with us."

Richard turned to look at the train and whispered under his breath, "Good to know. Maybe you won't be too upset if I take Caralyn out a few times. Caralyn probably doesn't tell you everything she does. At least I hope not."

Chapter Sixteen

"Mom, can I talk to you for a minute?" Caralyn asked as she walked into the living room.

"Of course you can, honey," Mom replied as she looked up from her chair and closed her book. "Is something troubling you?"

"You mean beside the fact I miss Tucker and even Derren for that matter."

"I know you miss the guys, but I can sense there is something else going on."

"I am bored out of my gourd with school. There's nothing to challenge me. I could do a better job teaching French than Miss Lemaire. I hate math with a passion. Biology isn't my thing. Mr. Green is the only teacher who challenges me and that's because he assigns me extra homework. He suggests topics for short stories, and I enjoy writing them. What should I do?"

"You could... what about..." Mom tried to think of something to diffuse the situation and get Caralyn's attention. She threw up her hands and said, "You and Nancy could double date."

"Seriously, Mom!" Caralyn stomped a foot. "That's your best suggestion. You know there aren't any boys in this town I would even consider dating. They are all so... boring and unsophisticated. Some of them are semi-good-looking, but I need more than that."

"Caralyn, I don't know what to tell you. You're passionate about sports. Maybe you should try for a part in the school play."

Caralyn slumped on the couch.

"Next year will be different, honey. Not only because of your classes, but also the social aspect of college."

"I'm looking forward to that."

Mom paused for a moment and then asked, "Have you given any more thought about Dickinson College?"

"I have considered it." Caralyn pulled her knees to her chest.

"Free tuition and books is quite an incentive. You could live on campus even though your father drives there every day."

"Mom, if Dad wasn't on the faculty there, I'm not sure I would even be considering Dickinson. Sure, the free tuition and stuff would make it easier on you guys."

Mom set her book on the end table, stood up and walked toward the kitchen. "Don't worry about that. You will probably get a full ride to Midwest Central, but if you don't, there is a clause in the trust. You can use the money for college."

Caralyn sprang from the couch and followed. "I'd rather not use that money unless it's an absolute necessity."

"I want you to enroll where you will be the happiest. I know Midwest Central has a good journalism program," Mom recalled. "Either way there will be someone to look after you."

Caralyn rolled her eyes.

"Your father at Dickinson and Tuck and Derren at Midwest Central." Mom pulled the ice tea from the fridge.

Caralyn hopped onto the countertop. "Mom! I'm not a child. I don't need anyone to check up on me every day."

Mom poured herself a glass of tea. "You're right. I forget how mature you are now."

"I know sarcasm when I hear it, Mom," Caralyn replied jumping down. "Sometimes I wish we didn't live in such a small town, but then I think about the things I love about this place. Like the fact everyone is friendly, and they help out in times of need."

Mom sensed part of Caralyn's frustrations resulted from her visit to Chicago to see Beth.

"Do you see yourself living in a large city after college?"

"In a way, I do, but I also can see myself living in a small town in a white house with a fence and flowers everywhere."

Mom hugged her.

"Thanks for listening. I feel better now. I told Mr. Green I would finish his latest assignment today. He let me choose the topic, and I thought of an idea."

"What did you choose?"

"I want to write a story about the twins I met earlier."

"That doesn't sound very challenging," Mom said adding sugar to her tea. "You've written other stories with more depth."

95

"I know, but it's just practice. It doesn't need to be Faulkner or Hemingway." She sat on her bed and thought about the morning she noticed two new kids outside the high school office.

"Hi, guys. Do you need help?"

"We're transferring in, and I guess we need to register."

"I can help you get started. I work in the office. I'm Caralyn Dawson by the way."

"I'm Blake Sullivan. This is Bruce. We moved here from Topeka, Kansas. We're sixteen and sophomores."

"I'm fifteen, but I'll be sixteen in November."

"Wow! That's great. Maybe we will have classes together and you can show us around."

"It's not a big school as you can see. It won't take you long to find your way around. I'm only fifteen, but I'm not a sophomore, I'm a senior."

"For real? You're joking, right?"

"No, I'm really a senior. I skipped a grade."

Bruce finally spoke. "When is your birthday?"

"November 30th."

"We are older than you, and yet you're two years ahead of us. How strange."

"I was really young when I started school." Caralyn opened a filing cabinet. "What brings you to our fine old town?"

"Our father is in the army, and he's going to be overseas for a year. We're living with Grandmother Sullivan. Mom passed away two years ago, and we can't stay with Dad this time so that's why we're here."

"I'm sorry about your Mom." Caralyn thought about telling the boys about her situation, but decided to wait for another time. "Here are some forms to get you started. Mrs. Brinkley will be here soon and she can do the rest. I'll try to find you guys at lunch and show you around if you want."

"That would be great." Bruce smiled and added, "We'll look for you."

One day, as they were heading to the cafeteria, Nancy Young asked Caralyn, "Why are you so nice to the Sullivan boys? They've just moved here this year, but you treat them like old friends."

"I guess I kinda feel sorry for them. They move around all the time because of their dad being in the army, and they lost their mother a couple years ago. Since I lost my mother, too, I feel sorry for them."

"Cara, you didn't lose your mother. I talked to her yesterday."

Caralyn stared at Nancy until she realized her mistake.

"I'm sorry, Cara, sometimes I forget the McKays aren't your real parents."

Caralyn grabbed a tray for herself and handed one to Nancy. "They are my real parents. They just aren't my biological parents."

"Thanks for the tray." Nancy looked at the choices for lunch. "Looks like meat loaf surprise again." She pretended to gag. "Do you remember anything about your birth mother?"

"No, I was only six-months-old when they were killed. There are pictures of her, and Mom said I look like her in some ways."

"Do you ever think about her, Cara? I know you love your Mom and all, but still you must wonder sometimes."

"Usually only when someone else brings it up. Normally I don't even think about it."

Nancy stopped moving and sounded miffed. "I'm sorry I brought it up, Cara. I'll try to remember not to in the future."

"Oh, it's all right. Don't be upset. I'm not, but please don't say anything to Bruce or Blake. I've never told them about my birth parents."

Nancy grabbed a carton of milk. "I never talk to them. Did you finish the story you were writing about them?"

"Yes, and I let Mr. Green read it."

"What did he say? Can I read it?"

"He said I could do better, so I threw it away. Sorry."

"That's okay." Nancy took a bite of meat loaf and grimaced. "I should have chosen a salad. They can't screw that up."

"Have you talked to Tucker lately?" Caralyn asked as she waved to Davey Stanfield.

"It's been a while."

"Should I get on his case? You still like him, right?"

"I like him, but he's busy at school. He said he wants to concentrate on basketball and school right now."

"He's such a jock." Caralyn made room for Davey. "What did you get?"

He pointed to his tray. "Whatever that's supposed to be."

"Throw it away," Nancy said.

He took a bite, shrugged and said, "It's probably not poisonous. What were you talking about?"

"Tucker hasn't talked to Nancy for a while."

"Did you break up?" Davey asked with a mouthful of meat loaf.

"Not exactly, but kinda," Nancy answered. "It's hard to know for sure. We never fought or anything."

"If you aren't going out with Tuck, would you want to see a show or eat dinner sometime?"

Caralyn elbowed him. "She's not interested in you, Davey. You told me you wanted to ask Melissa Shannon out. Did you?"

"I asked. She blew me off." He looked at Nancy again. "How about it?"

"I don't think so, Davey."

"Okay, are you gonna eat that?" he asked Caralyn.

She shook her head. "Help yourself."

"Happy birthday, honey. Sweet sixteen and never been kissed," Dad said kissing the top of her head.

"Dad! How do you know I've never been kissed?"

"Tucker doesn't count," he answered.

Caralyn flinched.

"He kisses you like a sister. Always has," Dad explained.

"Honey, you have been patient about waiting to date until this day," Mom said. "I know it hasn't been easy because all your classmates are older, and two of them are even engaged."

"It's okay, Mom. I haven't found to date anyone yet."

Dad mentioned, "Has anyone asked you to Homecoming?"

"A couple boys did, but I said no. I'm going with Tucker. He promised he would come home that weekend, and I'll have more fun with him."

Mom looked at Caralyn. "Does Tucker knows about going to Homecoming with you again?"

"I'll tell him soon."

"Now that you are sixteen I have one request."

"What, Daddy?"

"I want to meet any boys who take you on a date."

"That's fair enough."

"And you have to be home by your regular curfew..."

"I will..."

"And no parking on country roads and no letting boys kiss you and..."

"Daddy! You said you had only one rule."

"All right, maybe I have a few more rules."

"You don't need to worry. I'm not going to be doing any of those things. I'll wait until next year when I'm at college. There will be a lot more boys to choose from," she teased.

"That doesn't sound too reassuring, sweetie."

"I'm kidding. I didn't mean I'm going to go crazy and forget everything you taught me about right and wrong. I'm not going to be like Beth and leave home at the first chance I get. I still love living in our quaint little town."

"That's good to know." Mr. McKay glanced at his wife. "College already?"

Chapter Seventeen

One spring evening Caralyn asked her father, "Since I've had my license for two months now, would it be possible for me to use Tucker's car this Friday? There's a dance in Vernon Heights, and I'd like to go. May I use it, please?" She put her hands together like she was saying her nighttime prayers.

Dad removed his glasses and thought about her request. It seemed out of character for her to want to drive forty-five minutes to Vernon Heights. He told her, "I suppose you can use it, but only if you take a friend. Maybe Nancy or one of the other girls could go."

"Can I take the Sullivan twins? They will be moving away at the end of the school year, and I kinda promised them I would go somewhere with them."

Dad thought about it for a moment. He lifted his chin and asked. "Is this a date?"

"No!" She giggled and said, "I wouldn't be taking both of them on a date, Daddy." She didn't reveal she had been getting pressure from girls at school to find a boyfriend.

"All right, you can go with them," Dad said putting his glasses on again and picking up his newspaper. "They seem like good kids. Maybe you could ask Nancy to tag along."

"I asked her, but she has to work Friday night." She rested a hand on her hip. "It's not a double date, Daddy."

Friday night arrived, and Caralyn dressed in a pair of new, tight-fitting jeans, a white top and baby blue pullover sweater. She picked up the Sullivan twins, and they headed to Vernon Heights.

"Did you ever tell your parents why you are really going to this dance, Cara?" Bruce asked from the passenger seat.

She slowed the Civic around a corner but not enough as the tires squealed. "No, and you better never tell anyone either."

"We won't tell," Blake promised. "What are we supposed to do if you get sick and start puking?"

"I just want to drink one beer. That won't make me sick."

"Maybe, but you better be careful. This guy who's giving you the beer might want something in return."

"I'm not giving him anything. Not even a smile."

They arrived in Vernon Heights and parked in the lot next to the pavilion. She made the Sullivan boys pay for the entrance tickets. They could hear the deep throb of the bass guitar as they entered the concrete block, metal-roofed building. They looked around and Caralyn saw Ronnie dancing with two girls.

"There he is." She pointed him out to Bruce and Blake. "Mike showed me a photo. His nose looks like a bird's beak."

"That's the guy who buys beer for underage kids, huh? He looks like a loser if you ask me," Blake said.

"He is a loser, but I want to try a beer. Beth wouldn't give me any the last time I saw her. She told me I was a baby."

"So you want to prove her wrong, huh?" Bruce asked.

"What can it hurt to try it?"

She danced with the Sullivan brothers while keeping an eye on Ronnie.

"It's too warm for this sweater. Will you hold it for me while I talk to him?" She pulled it over her head, handed it to Bruce and walked toward Ronnie between songs.

"Hi, do you remember me?"

He took a puff on his Camel, coughed and answered in a raspy voice, "Nope. Never seen you before. What do you want?"

"I'm Caralyn," she hollered as the band began the next song. "You said you would let me have a beer. Actually, Mike Mulvaney told me you would buy it."

He checked her out. "How old are you anyway?" he yelled. "You look too young to even get in here. Are you like twelve?"

"I'm sixteen. I know you bought beer for Mike and his friends."

"That's too bad. Sixteen is still jailbait. No way I'm giving you a beer now or ever. Go away and stop bothering me."

His remark took her by surprise, so she responded by teasing him. "I will let you make out with me and maybe even more if you buy beer for me and my friends."

Ronnie laughed bitterly, leaned close to her ear, poked her breast and sneered, "Listen, kid, I said to bug off. You must think I'm pretty stupid. Ain't no way I'm buying beer for babies with all the cops in Vernon Heights trying to nail my ass. Either you leave now, or I will tell the cops you offered sex for money. That's called prostitution if you don't know. Scram!"

This startled her, but she pretended it didn't bother her. She did an about-face. Ronnie grabbed her butt as she started to walk away.

She pivoted, slapped him and screamed, "Don't you ever do that again!"

The Sullivan twins took two steps forward, ready to attack him. Caralyn looked at them and held up her hand to make sure they didn't do anything. Caralyn clenched her fists in anger as she walked away.

"Caralyn, are you all right? We heard what that jerk said to you. Do you want us to punch him out?"

"No, don't do anything like that. You will get in trouble, and I don't want that to happen. Let's dance for a while and then head home. I don't care about the beer anymore. He really is a bastard. She took one last look at Ronnie and gave him the finger though he wasn't looking.

After a couple dances with both twins, she looked around trying to spot Ronnie. "I want to get out of here."

"If you're looking for that loser, he left a few minutes ago with some girl."

"I wasn't looking for him," she said without much conviction. "I can wait until I'm older to have a beer."

On the way home Caralyn let Blake drive, since he now had his driver's license.

"That guy was a total stoner," Bruce said.

"Yeah, we saw him touch you right there out in the open. I thought he was going to put his hand inside your shirt for a moment," Blake said as he kept his eyes straight ahead.

"I wanted to pound him," Bruce added.

"I thought I might have to knee him in the balls for a second. He caught me off guard. I would never let him touch me. I hope he gets busted."

"He's probably been busted before," Bruce said.

"I'm not ready to go home," Caralyn said. "I know a place where we can talk and watch the stars. It's such a gorgeous night. Let's stop and get a six pack first though."

"A six pack! Where are we gonna get beer?" Bruce asked. "You thought that creep could buy some for you and look how that ended up."

"Not beer," Caralyn said. "Pop. I want either Coke or Dr Pepper."

They stopped at a gas station, and the guys bought the pop and snacks.

"So where is this place we're going?" Blake asked as they got back in the car.

Caralyn opened a can of Dr Pepper and pointed. "Keep following this road out of town, and I'll tell you where to turn."

Blake followed her directions, and she had him turn into a field Uncle Alton owned. "Where are we?" he asked.

"See that strange little building over there?"

"Yeah, what is it?" Blake asked as he parked close to it.

"It's a wooden shed built into the side of the hill with a sloping metal roof. Uncle Alton stores hay for his cattle there. I like to climb on the roof." She hopped out of the car. "Come on guys. Let's gaze at the stars for awhile." She ran up the hill and jumped across the open space to the roof. She stood on the far edge about ten feet off the ground and looked up into the sky. "Here I am world! Does anybody care?"

She sat on the roof's edge with her feet dangling in the air as the Sullivans joined her. They watched the stars, and she let the boys get close as they talked about school.

"Will you guys stop staring at my breasts. You are acting like you have x-ray vision or something."

"We aren't staring at you, Caralyn," Blake said, "But it's normal for guys our age to be curious."

"Will you guys behave? I can't pretend we were not friends and let you do something."

They talked as they drank the pop and ate the snacks. She could feel their hips against hers but didn't react. They kept looking at her legs and chest. Bruce's eyes pleaded for more intimacy.

"Stop it! I'm not going to let you touch me."

"We would never tell anyone if you let us." Bruce made another attempt.

"It ain't gonna happen, so let it go!" Caralyn said with enough anger in her voice to convince the boys not to press the issue.

They sat on the edge of the roof and finished the pop without any more conversation. The boys stood up and walked to the other end, jumped back onto the hill and sat down.

Caralyn stood up and shouted, "I wanted to taste some beer. Is that such a terrible thing to do?"

"We don't think so, Cara."

"You guys are too nice to me." She stood with her arms outstretched. She was facing away from the boys as she hollered, "Here I am world! I'm ready to grow up and no one cares."

"We care, Caralyn."

She didn't respond as she walked to the other end of the roof, wiped away the dirt, sat and moved onto her back.

"You have been good friends to me all year, and it's probably best we weren't able to get any beer."

Blake and Bruce moved close to her. Bruce put a hand on her stomach, but she swatted it away. She stretched her arms above her head and closed her eyes.

"Have you ever seen a boy naked, Caralyn?" Blake asked. He stared at her chest and put a hand on her leg.

She pushed his hand away after a few seconds and turned to face him. "How can you ask such a personal question? No! Never, and I don't want to. I hope you two aren't going to try anything stupid because that would ruin our friendship."

Both guys got up and took a step away from her.

104

"Have you ever made out with a boy, Cara?"

"Just once." She held out a hand and Bruce helped her up.

"Who was it? We won't tell anyone. How far did you let him go?" Bruce asked.

"If you must know, it was Tucker McKay."

"Caralyn, isn't he your brother?" Blake asked.

"No! He's not my brother. I am kinda adopted. My birth parents were killed in a car crash when I was a baby."

"What a bummer. Why didn't you ever tell us before?" Blake asked.

"It happened so long ago, and I know how much you miss your Mom, so I didn't want to say anything."

"You could have told us," Bruce said. "We always wondered why your last name is Dawson. I guess we must be pretty dumb not to realize something was different."

Blake touched her jeans from behind.

"Blake, you promised you would behave."

"I know. Sorry, Cara. I was thinking about your cute butt."

"Stop it!" she warned but grinned at the same time.

"We should get going, Caralyn."

"What time is it?"

"It's after midnight."

"Oh crap! I will get killed." She sprinted to the car.

"We'll get you home as quick as we can," Blake said.

They got back into town in less than ten minutes.

"Pull into Grandma's driveway," she instructed. "Park next to the house. You can crash here tonight."

Caralyn had the boys stay next door at Grandma's house rather than drive them the ten miles to their grandmother's farm.

Chapter Eighteen

Caralyn woke up when she heard Mom in the kitchen. She quickly put on a pair of shorts and a t-shirt.

"What time did you get home last night, Caralyn?"

"I'm sorry, Mom. I know it after my curfew."

"Well, as long as you are all right, I guess your father won't ground you for too long. Maybe only a week."

"Okay, I deserve it. I let the Sullivan twins sleep next door since it was so late. I should check on them."

She hustled next door to see if the guys were awake. She walked into the bedroom and both boys were sound asleep on top of the beds in only their underwear. She looked at them and grinned. *White underwear. So typical.* She jumped when Bruce began to stir and opened his eyes.

"Morning, Caralyn. I had a dream about you."

"Good morning, Bruce," she said avoiding looking at his underwear. "Was it a good dream?"

"Very good, or maybe very bad, depending on your point of view. I dreamed I saw you naked, and we kissed and you wanted me to make love to you."

She smacked his arm. "That was a nightmare, and it will never happen. I should let you guys get dressed. I wanted to see if you were all right. I can make eggs if you are hungry. Do you want some?"

"Sure, that would be great."

"Get dressed and meet me in the kitchen." She took one more look at their underwear before leaving.

The boys sat at the table as she fixed breakfast.

"Caralyn, do you regret what happened last night?"

"I don't regret it. I'm too young to drink anything stronger than pop." She paused for a moment as she viciously scrambled the eggs as if that action would hurt Ronnie. She turned back to the boys. "Blake, stop staring at my breasts. I'm still not going to let you see them."

"It was quite a night after all."

106

She scooped the eggs onto plates and handed one to each boy. Bruce leered at her long enough to make her uncomfortable.

"Are you trying to imagine how I looked in your dream?"

"Yeah, I admit it. Do you want to get undressed and let us see you naked?"

"No! Would you like me to crack your head like I did the eggs?" She waved the frying pan at him. "What if Mom or Dad caught me. I would be grounded for life." She looked out the kitchen window. "They are in the yard."

"Are you wearing a bra, Caralyn?"

"Yes, why?"

"I thought that if you weren't..."

"You are so bad. Shame on you." She teased them by lifting her t-shirt to show them her bra for a split second before covering up.

"Please let us see them, Caralyn," they begged.

Caralyn thought about it as she looked out the window to see if Mom was still outside, but she didn't see her. "All right. But just for a second." She lifted her t-shirt up.

Right then Mom walked in the kitchen and saw her with her t-shirt pulled up. "Caralyn Ann! What in heaven's name are you doing? Cover yourself this instant!"

"Sorry, Mom. I was only going to..."

"I don't want to hear it, young lady. Get back to the house and stay in your room." Mom McKay pointed toward the house and then turned to face the boys. "As for you two, I think you had best leave as soon as you finish your breakfast."

"Yes, Mrs. McKay. We're sorry, but Caralyn didn't do anything." They gulped down the eggs.

"I will be the judge of that. I think you should stay away from Caralyn for a while."

"Yes, Ma'am. We'll walk home."

Mom McKay faced them with her hands on her hips for a time. "Don't be ridiculous. Caralyn can take you home. Wait here until I come back. I need to talk to her."

Mom found Caralyn sitting on her bed crying.

"I'm so sorry, Mom. I didn't mean to do anything, but I got carried away." Caralyn wiped her eyes with her hand.

"Caralyn, you are growing up, and I know I haven't talked to you about sex and boys much. I wish I had. Boys your age are obviously curious, and they will try to get you to do things maybe you don't want to and really shouldn't until you are older."

"I didn't let them see me, Mom. I only let them see my bra."

"Cara, I heard what they asked you to do, and it looked like you were going to do it. If I hadn't walked in the room, you might have let them see more than your bra."

Caralyn started to cry again because she knew Mom was right. "Are you going to tell Daddy what I did?"

Mom thought about it and decided. "No, honey, I'm not going to tell him. It will be our secret as long as the Sullivan boys keep their mouths shut."

Caralyn hugged her. "I'm sorry if I disappointed you. I'll try to behave better."

"Caralyn, I love you so much, and I always will. Try to remember boys will be after you because you are so pretty and their hormones are out of control."

"I will, Mom."

"You need to run the boys home, but I want you to come right back."

"I will. I won't even get out of the car. I might just slow down and make them jump out," she said with a grin.

"Slow down quite a bit," Mom said.

On the ride out to the farm Caralyn asked, "Why are you guys being so quiet?"

"I guess because we got you in trouble," Bruce answered. "Do you think your parents will ground you for long?"

"If I had to guess, I would say two weeks. I've done worse and never been grounded for longer than that."

Blake shook his head and then laughed. "I don't think your mom wants to ever see us again."

"Don't worry about it. I'll be all right," she said and then giggled. "I did act pretty naughty." She looked at the guys jeans and remembered how they looked in their underwear. *I saw more of you guys than you saw of me.*

"All you did was let us see your bra. We don't think you should be punished too harshly."

"Hey, Cara, since you're already in trouble, how about you let us see your bra again?"

"You're lucky I'm driving right now, Blake Sullivan, or else I would pound you."

She returned from the Sullivan farm, and Dad talked to her, "Caralyn, I know what time you got home last night. I will give you a choice of either being grounded for a week, or else cleaning up the garage and basement of Grandma Florence's house. Your choice."

Caralyn wasted no time before answering, "I will clean the house and garage. I'm sorry I lost track of time last night, Daddy."

"It's okay," Dad told her as she kissed him and gave him a hug. "You are usually good about being home before your curfew."

Caralyn changed into a red sports bra and an old t-shirt to work on Grandma's house. As she cleaned, she paused to look at the pictures still hanging on the walls. She took one off the wall and looked at it closely. She knew this was the last picture ever taken of her parents. She placed it back on the wall before her eyes filled with tears. She cleaned the house and started on the garage.

Mom walked toward the garage as Caralyn tossed an old box into the garbage can on the side of the white garage.

"We are going to Butler. Do you want anything special from the store, honey?"

"Could you bring home chips and Dr Pepper, please."

"Anything else?"

"May I have ice cream?"

"You know your father will make sure he has ice cream."

Caralyn kept working in the humid, stifling air of the garage. She decided to take off her t-shirt. Though she kept the garage door open, no one could see her as she worked up a sweat. She was determined to clean up the garage as best she could. As she finished she heard a car pull into the driveway at the McKay house. She assumed Mom and Dad had returned and stood by the open door in her sports bra and shorts admiring her work. She walked toward Grandma's back porch and saw Mr. Young and Nancy in the McKay's driveway. She stood still for a moment as he looked at her. She scampered into the garage and slipped on her t-shirt.

"Hi, Nancy. Hello, Mr. Young. I didn't know you were coming. Mom and Dad drove into Butler to do the grocery shopping. They should be back soon."

"That's all right, Caralyn. I need to drop off this check for the church. Will you make sure your father gets it?." He stared at her and shook his head.

"Yes, of course, Mr. Young."

As they drove away, he warned Nancy, "I hope you and your sister will never embarrass me by displaying yourself the way Caralyn did. It must be the influence of her older sister."

"We will both behave, Dad, and I'm sure Caralyn didn't realize you were here or else she would have kept her shirt on."

Later that evening, Mr. Young called and talked to Mr. McKay. "She came out of the garage without her shirt on. I wanted to let you know what occurred and voice my disapproval. I know I would want to be informed if my girls ever did something so inappropriate."

"Thank you for calling, and I will talk to Caralyn. I'm sorry it happened." Dad shook his head, walked to her room and knocked on the door.

"Come in."

He stood in the door with a frown. "Cara, I spoke to Mr. Young on the phone. He told me what he saw and he sounded clearly upset. Is it true?"

She sat up on her bed. "Daddy, I was working in the garage, and I got so hot and sweaty." She waved her hands and then pretended to wipe sweat from her forehead. "I took off my t-shirt and finished cleaning the garage in my sports bra and shorts. After I got done I was walking to the porch. I didn't know he or Nancy were there until I saw him, and as soon as I did I raced into the garage and put on my t-shirt. I'm sorry I let him see me like that, but you've seen me in that sports bra. I've even worn it without any other top for a run. No one ever made a big deal about it before."

He moved to the edge of her bed. "Just between you and me, honey, I think Mr. Young is making a fuss because he likes to point out people's faults. That doesn't mean I think it's all right for you to be walking around in your underwear, but I can understand why it happened. Please be more careful in the future, okay?"

"I will. I really didn't know they were here. I heard a car pull up, but I thought it was you and Mom."

"By the way, honey, the garage and house look so much better. Thank you for all your hard work."

"You're welcome, Daddy. I'd rather do a few hours of hard labor than to be grounded for a week."

"Caralyn, I'm so sorry Daddy called your father," Nancy whispered over the phone. "Are you in big trouble?"

"Not really," Caralyn said then decided to tease her. "Just the usual talk about not encouraging boys by walking around in my underwear."

"Tell me you've never done that," Nancy said.

"I'm kidding. Daddy told me not to do it again."

Nancy hung up and Caralyn plopped onto her bed and talked to her teddy bear, "What would Nancy's father say about swimming at Grandma and Grandpa's pond? He would bust a gut if he knew."

111

"We need to narrow the choices to two or three. We will have two weeks at the most, and we will be able to stay at motels as long as we can find reasonably priced ones," Dad informed Tucker and Caralyn as they sat in the living room to plan a much needed summer vacation.

Tucker and Caralyn discussed their options and Tucker asked, "What about renting a cabin in the mountains in Tennessee? We found several that look interesting. There is this one on the side of a hill with woods all around and a lake close by."

"Don't you think you might get bored. What would you be doing all day?"

"We could go hiking and swimming and stuff," Caralyn answered. "It would be cheaper than staying at motels. We can do our own cooking and it's close enough to Smoky Mountain National Park so we could spend time there. We could take our bicycles."

"What do you think, Sarah? It might not be a real vacation for you if you cook and clean like normal."

"I think it sounds wonderful. I would get bored if I didn't do some cooking, and Cara can help me."

They decided to rent the cabin for one week, and then take their time getting home; stopping at interesting sites as they made their way back to Stockton Woods.

The departure day arrived, and everyone rose early. The packing had been done the night before, so after breakfast, they hit the road.

"We should be able to get there late this evening if we don't make a lot of stops," Dad said.

Tucker helped Dad with the driving and even Caralyn drove for a short stretch of Interstate. With minimal stops they made good time and finally reached their destination.

"The keys are supposed to be in this box on the door, and I know the combination."

"This deck looks new," Tucker said. "You can still smell the wood."

"Please hurry, Daddy! I've got to go so bad!" Caralyn hopped from one foot to the other.

"Cara, you can use that tree over there if you can't wait," Tucker said to annoy her.

"Tucker, don't tease Caralyn. You promised to behave and get along."

"We will, Mom. You know we like to tease each other though."

"There! Got the keys." Dad held them up.

He opened the front door, and Caralyn rushed inside. She found the bathroom, and everyone else checked out the cabin. Except for the bedrooms, at opposite ends of the cabin, and the one bathroom, the cabin's interior opened into one large room. The backside featured a full-width covered porch with a great view of the mountains.

Tucker checked it out. "Hey, Cara! There's a hot tub out here and it's running!"

She stepped out to see for herself. "Look at the view, Tuck. It's great!"

Mom and Dad checked out the bedrooms and called for the kids to come and see.

Mom pointed to one side, "That will be our room." She did an about-face. "These will be your rooms."

"Cara, two bedrooms! I won't have to sleep on the couch."

"The rooms are small, but you only need them for sleeping," Mom said.

"It will be fine, Mom. I had a nightmare last night that I might have to share a bed with him. This is perfect."

Mom and Dad vanished to the back porch leaving Tucker and Caralyn in their rooms.

Caralyn smiled at Tucker. "Which room do you want, Tuck? I don't really have a preference."

"I'll take this one. Sit by me." He patted a spot. "I want to talk about what we should do. Hiking and swimming are obvious."

She sat next to him. "We are going to have so much fun, Tuck. I can't wait to go hiking. Will you promise to keep a lookout for wild animals. I don't want to get eaten by a bear."

"Don't worry, Carrie. Bears won't want to eat you. There's no meat on your bones." He tickled her side as he teased her. "Come on. Let's start unloading the car."

After supper that night, Tucker and Caralyn decided to go for a hike. The sun still provided enough light, so they headed to the lake, about a quarter of a mile away.

"It looks picturesque and the water is cool, but not too cold for swimming," Tucker said as he stuck his hand in the water.

Caralyn smiled and giggled.

"What's so funny, Cara?"

"Picturesque?"

"You're not the only member of this family with a fancy vocabulary. I may not be a wannabe writer like you, but I still know a few fancy words."

"Do you wanna go skinny dipping since there isn't anyone around?" She touched the buttons of her top.

"Carrie! How can you be thinking of such a thing?"

"I think it would be fun. Are you afraid to let me see you naked? Afraid I might make fun of your little thing," Caralyn pointed at him and then giggled.

Tucker grabbed her, tossed her over his shoulder and swatted her bottom lightly.

"I was only teasing. I know it's not little so put me down, and stop smacking my butt unless you plan on doing something."

Tucker set her down. They looked at each other and then at the water. "How would we get dry? How would we explain being wet when we got back to the cabin? Mom knows we didn't bring suits with us on our hike. She would know we went skinny dipping."

Caralyn grinned. "Mom knows about me skinny dipping at Grandma's pond. I told her about it, and I told her you and Derren saw me naked."

"Carrie! Why did you tell Mom? Did she tell Dad?"

"She didn't tell Dad, but I wanted to tell her. She told me I shouldn't let you or Derren see me like that anymore because you guys are too old and because I'm a young lady." She grinned at Tucker. "But it wouldn't bother me if you see me naked again."

He stared at her and tried not to think of how that would excite him.

"We can't tonight," Tucker said as he motioned for her to get on his back.

She whispered in his ear, "Does that mean we can later in the week?"

"Why do you want to skinny dip so bad? If Mom or Dad find out they will ground us both, and will probably send us home."

"I think it will be fun. You have seen me naked, so I don't have anything to hide, and I've seen your thing when it was big. You don't need to be shy in front of me."

Tucker came to an immediate stop and set her down. "What? When? Are you making that up to embarrass me?"

She nodded and asked, "Are you embarrassed?"

He ignored her for a moment.

"Caralyn, would you go skinny dipping with other boys around?"

"Just you and Derren. I wouldn't want anyone else to see me. Are you shy about letting me see you, Tuck? You don't need to be. Do all boys look the same? I've never seen anyone else. I almost saw Derren one time when he was taking a leak by the pond, and he didn't know I was there."

"I guess most guys look pretty much the same. I never gave it much thought."

"It doesn't mean you're gay if you see someone's penis, Tucker. I would sometimes look at other girls in the shower after gym class. Girls come in all different sizes, you know. Some have big breasts, and others have smaller ones. Butts come in many different sizes and shapes."

"Caralyn, please stop talking about naked girls."

115

"Why? Are you getting big?"

"No! I don't want to hear about this."

"Have you seen Nancy's breasts? I have."

Tucker turned red because Caralyn was talking about Nancy Young whom he had dated and really liked. "Stop it, Caralyn, before I toss you in the lake with your clothes on."

Caralyn stopped teasing him, and they kept hiking. Dusk settled over the area before they got back to the cabin.

"Where did you go? Mom and I were about to look for you. We thought maybe a bear ate you, Caralyn." Dad laughed as he teased her. "Mom and I are going for a walk to the lake and watch the stars. We are taking a flashlight, so we don't get lost."

"Have fun," Tucker said.

Caralyn wanted to get ready for bed, so she got her pajamas out of the suitcase and changed while Tucker sat on the couch and read a magazine. She and Tucker were both sound asleep when Mom and Dad returned from the lake.

Caralyn and Tucker used a canoe to explore the lake the next morning. They spotted a couple of newer-looking cabins on the opposite shore, and saw a few people, but no other kids. Mom and Dad escaped to go hiking, and they all met for lunch.

"How was the lake?" Dad asked.

"Bigger than we thought. My arms are sore. Tucker made me do all the rowing. He didn't help at all."

Dad grinned at her. "For some reason I find that difficult to believe, Cara."

"Well, he should have done all the rowing, so I could relax and work on my tan."

"There are a few cabins around, but not many, and we didn't see any other teenagers," Tucker added.

"You can keep each other company."

After dinner that night, Mom and Dad planned to use the hot tub.

"We are going swimming in the lake," Caralyn announced. "There is a spot that's not too deep close by the dock."

"Be careful, Caralyn, and don't swim too far from shore. Tucker, make sure she stays close."

"I will, Mom. I'll tie a rope around her if I need to."

Caralyn put her bathing suit on under her shorts and t-shirt. Tucker wore his trunks and a t-shirt. They headed to the lake and didn't see anyone else around. Tucker took of his t-shirt and jumped in feet first off the small dock.

"The water's not very deep here, Cara. Don't dive in headfirst."

She removed her t-shirt and shorts. She looked around, didn't see anyone and removed her bikini top. Tucker had his back to her as she got in the water.

She swam to Tucker and asked. "Are you going to take off your trunks?"

"No!" He looked closer at Caralyn. "Did you already take your suit off, Carrie?"

"Just my top. There's no one around to see us, Tuck."

He looked around and didn't see a light anywhere. "Don't take anything else off."

"No one could see anything if I did."

"Just don't, Caralyn." Tucker grabbed her and slung her over his shoulder like a sack of potatoes. She giggled as he held her there.

"Are you trying to feel up my butt, Tuck?"

"I should smack your butt for taking off your top."

She squealed as he lightly touched her. "I'm telling!"

"Go ahead! Who are you going to tell?"

They swam for a while longer then sat beside each other on the dock with Caralyn still topless.

"I like swimming here better than at Uncle Alton's lake. Can we do it again before we leave?"

"I suppose we can go swimming every day if you want, Carrie."

"That's not what I mean, and you know it."

"We'll see about the skinny dipping. There might be other people coming, and we might not have another chance."

117

"Then I'm going back in the water." She jumped in and splashed his legs.

"Stay close to the dock, Caralyn."

"I will."

Tucker put his t-shirt on and a couple of minutes later Mom and Dad walked up to the wooden dock and saw him.

Mom asked, "Tucker, where's Caralyn?"

Tucker was surprised to see his parents. *Uh oh! This could be trouble for Carrie.* "She's right there, Mom."

Caralyn saw Mom and Dad and froze in position.

Mom noticed her bikini top on the dock. "Caralyn, what are you doing? Put your clothes on right now."

Embarrassed and near tears, Caralyn covered her breasts with her arms, but Dad had already seen her.

"Caralyn Ann, put your top back on."

"I will if you turn around, Daddy." Dad turned around so Caralyn could get out of the water and put her top back on.

Mom scolded Tucker, "Why did you let her do that? Oh, never mind."

"Mom, don't be mad at Tucker. It was my idea. He tried to stop me, but he was already in the water so he couldn't."

Dad covered his eyes with a hand and started to chuckle.

Mom glared at him. "What is so funny about our daughter being almost naked in the lake?"

"Nothing, but I remember a time when a couple of young people did the same thing many years ago."

Mom turned deep red as Tucker and Caralyn listened.

"Mom! Did you and Daddy go skinny dipping?" Caralyn shouted incredulously.

"That's different, and it was a long time ago."

"Were you already married?" Caralyn asked.

Dad put his arms around his wife and hugged her. "No, we were in college."

"Jim! You shouldn't tell them about... oh, never mind."

Tucker and Caralyn looked at each other amazed that Mom and Dad were not any different than real people.

"Come on, honey. Let's walk back to the cabin and let the kids have their fun. Don't stay out too late and be careful." Dad advised as he and Mom headed back to the cabin. "And keep your suit on, young lady. That's an order."

Caralyn and Tucker sat on the dock and stared at each other without saying a word. After a moment they started laughing.

"Who would have ever guessed?" Tucker shrugged.

"Do you think Daddy saw me?" Caralyn asked while putting on her shorts and t-shirt.

"I don't know."

"I don't care if Mom saw, but I don't want to think Daddy saw me topless."

"Don't worry. You are still his innocent little girl, and I'm sure you can still get him to do whatever you want."

"I'm not a spoiled brat, am I, Tuck?"

"Oh, you most definitely are, Caralyn. No doubt about it."

At breakfast the next morning Caralyn fidgeted in her seat and picked at her food.

"Are you all right, Cara? You usually like hash browns."

"I'm fine, Daddy. I guess I'm a little embarrassed about last night. Am I going to be grounded?"

"No, you are not grounded, or in trouble. I know you've been skinny dipping before with Tucker, and, no, Mom didn't tell me. I overheard you and Mom talking about swimming at the pond."

"Daddy, do you think I was acting especially naughty?"

He massaged the back of his neck. "I like to think you were enjoying some innocent fun and it will never happen again."

Caralyn had something else she wanted to ask but was nervous about asking. She looked at Tucker.

"Dad, Cara is wondering if you saw her naked. Did you?"

Caralyn hit Tucker's arm with some force behind it.

"What? You want to know, but you're too shy to ask."

Dad answered, "No, honey, I didn't. I saw you weren't wearing your top, but that's all."

119

"Do you still love me?"

"I will always love you, Caralyn. No matter what you do, and you will always be my little girl, too. Even when you are old with kids of your own."

Caralyn hugged Dad and kissed his cheek.

"Caralyn, you are so spoiled!" Tucker rolled his eyes.

Tucker and Caralyn dashed to the lake for a morning swim after breakfast.

"It feels like the water is warmer today, Tuck."

"Maybe a little, but it's also ten degrees hotter."

They played in the water and Tucker tossed Caralyn around, and she squealed with delight.

One time as Tucker grabbed Caralyn from behind, his hands ended up on her bikini top and it shifted.

He let go. "Ooops! Sorry, Carrie. I didn't mean for that to happen."

She looked at her bikini top. "No biggie. Nothing you haven't touched before."

Caralyn fixed her top and they continued swimming. Tucker set her on his shoulder and carried her until he released her in the shallow water. She turned away from Tucker and wiggled her bottom.

"Do I have a nice butt, Tucker?" She climbed onto the dock.

Tucker joined her. "Your butt is enormous."

"Not funny." Caralyn pushed Tucker off the dock into the shallow water. He grabbed her ankle and pulled her into the water.

She smacked Tucker and he grabbed her around her waist as she tried to get away. She squirmed for a moment but then stopped.

"We need to stop, Carrie," Tucker said.

She looked at his trunks and giggled. "Did I cause that?"

He ignored her and they headed back to the cabin after Caralyn put on her shorts and t-shirt.

That night as Mom and Dad frolicked in the hot tub, Caralyn read a book on the couch. Tucker listened to his iPod on the chair.

"Hey, Tuck." When he didn't answer, she tossed a throw pillow at him.

He removed his earbuds. "What?"

"I'm not sorry for what I did to... you know. Does that make me a bad girl?"

"Yes. You are very bad, Caralyn."

"Do you like it when I am bad, Tuck? I could be dreadfully bad if you want me to."

"You better behave, Caralyn, and lower your voice before Mom hears you talking about what happened. We would both be in trouble if they find out you were topless again."

"It was your fault my top slipped. I didn't take my top off like the other day."

"Sorry, I didn't do it on purpose."

After they got back to Stockton Woods, Mom noticed Tucker and Caralyn became almost inseparable. She also realized they didn't fight like when they were kids, and didn't tease each other as much.

"Derren, why do we always load hay into the loft when it's a hundred degrees out?" Tucker asked wiping sweat out of his eyes.

Derren shrugged then tossed another hay bale up to Tucker. "I hate wearing these flannel shirts, but I guess it's better than having our arms scratched raw."

Caralyn worked at the Stanfield farm as often as the guys. She helped Grandma in the garden and with canning and pickling. After working all day, the kids would head to the pond to cool off.

"You have to keep your top on, Carrie," Tucker warned.

"Don't worry. I'm not going to get naked in front of you guys. I want to work on my tan while the sun's still out."

"You're tanner than I've ever seen," Davey said.

121

"I've been wearing my bikini top while I help Grandma."

Davey edged closer to her and whispered, "I don't care if you take off your top."

She dug her elbow into his ribs. "Don't even joke about it. Tucker would get mad if I did."

"You used to when we were kids."

"Key word being kids. Little kids, Davey. Like five or six."

Mom saw them kissing on Grandma Florence's back porch one day as Caralyn sat on Tucker's lap. When Caralyn placed his hand on her breast, Mom had a meltdown and yelled, "Tucker James McKay! Caralyn Ann Dawson!"

"Caralyn, get down! Mom's coming and she's furious." He nudged her and she fell off the porch to the ground.

"What is going on?"

"Mom..."

Mom pointed to the house. "Your room! Now!"

Caralyn drifted far enough around Mom to avoid getting swatted. "It was my fault," she shouted over her shoulder.

Mom glared at Tucker.

"Sorry, Mom."

"Not good enough. I know you know better than to... I don't know." She put a hands to her ears and shook her head. "I am too upset to even know what to say. She's your sister."

"No, she's not," Tucker insisted. "She is not my real sister."

"Okay, not technically, but you've grown up together," Mom said. She took a deep breath, closed her eyes and muttered, "How could this happen?" She opened her eyes and looked at Tucker. "People think she is."

"No they don't. Everyone knows about the accident, and how she lived with Grandma."

"I think of you as brother and sister."

"I can't help that," he replied.

"Do not cop an attitude." She pointed a finger. "I love you both the same."

"Sorry, but you called her Caralyn Dawson just now."

122

Mom took a deep breath, and waited before she said, "You love each other, and I am afraid you aren't old enough to handle the emotions and..."

"I'm not going to sleep with her, Mom."

"Kissing leads to more and more."

"Not always."

"Hah! I was once your age, and I know better."

Caralyn walked back and stood at the edge of the house. "He's not my brother, and I know the difference, Mom."

"I saw what you did. That's being too intimate at your age."

"Have you forgotten about us swimming at the lake?"

"No, and if I thought for one second it would lead to this, we would have come home right then. I know this isn't the first time you've kissed each other, but I tried to convince myself you were being curious."

"Are you going to tell Daddy?" Caralyn asked.

Mom rolled her shoulders to relieve the tension. "I'm afraid to. He will explode at both of you. Will you promise not to... I don't even know what to call it."

"We won't kiss each other anymore, Mom," Tucker said.

"Do I need to make you stay at the farm for the rest of the summer? I can't watch you every moment."

"I could stay with Beth," Caralyn said.

"No!" Mom said. "I blame her for talking about sex..."

"I was curious like everyone my age," Caralyn said. "It doesn't mean I'm going to..."

"Don't even say it, young lady. You don't know what you would let someone do because you've never been in that situation."

"I'm not too weak to defend myself."

"You are no match for a man when it comes to strength."

"Could we continue this in the house?" Tucker asked.

Caralyn laughed. "You get so embarrassed if we bring up sex. You weren't shy about kissing Nancy."

"I didn't know about that." Mom furrowed her brow.

"Mom are you still upset because of what happened when the Sullivans crashed here?"

Mom thought for a moment then sighed. "That didn't help. I might have been remembering what you did."

Tucker looked at Caralyn then his mother. "What are you talking about? What did you do, Cara?"

"None of your business," she answered. "I know it doesn't matter, but when I kissed Tuck, I knew he wouldn't try anything else. If I kissed Blake or Bruce, they would have wanted more."

"I have no idea how to handle this," Mom said. She rubbed her temples and took a deep breath. "I can't ground you. I can't make you stay with Beth. I could make Tucker stay at the farm."

"I've been working there a lot. I could sleep there."

"How will you explain it to Daddy?" Caralyn asked.

"No clue. He will be too confused and incensed to make a rational decision."

"If it helps, I confess I like kissing Tuck, but partly because there's no one else in town I would consider sexy. But there are lots of guys at college."

Tucker shook his head. "Somehow I don't think that helps, Carrie."

"I will not mention this to your father if you promise not to let it happen again."

"It won't," Tucker said.

Caralyn didn't answer.

Chapter Twenty

Caralyn watched as Tucker shot free throws at the hoop attached to the garage. She tossed him the basketball and smiled. "Tuck, I am so excited we will be together at school. I missed you so much last year."

He stopped his shot and held the ball. His face was clearly serious as he mentioned, "I don't know how to tell you this, but I'm transferring to a school in California."

"What? No, you're not! You're teasing me." She rushed over and grabbed the ball out of his hands. "Don't you want me to hang out with you guys?" She tried to shoot the ball.

He blocked her shot and then turned around to grab the ball. "I suppose it will be all right."

"Creep!" She pushed him in the back. "You're afraid to admit you missed me last year."

"Did not," Tucker swished a jump shot.

"Did so. Derren told me you whined about not having me there."

"If you need anything, anything at all, you can call us, honey. I'm sure it will take time for you to adjust to college life." Mom sighed as she looked at Caralyn. "I can't believe you are going to college already. Remember there are plenty of older guys who might want to take advantage of a young girl."

"Mom! I'm not a child and besides, Tucker and Derren are here. They will protect me."

Mom wondered if she would need protection from Tucker. She hadn't mentioned anything to Dad about the kids' new feelings for each other.

"Remember to call us twice a week, Caralyn, and keep your door locked all the time. There are boys on the same floor so be careful." Mom hugged her and didn't try to keep from crying. "Remember to... I don't know. Be safe."

Tucker grinned and said, "You didn't cry last year when you brought me up here."

"That's because they love me more than you," Caralyn teased.

Dad McKay patted Tucker's back and then squeezed Caralyn tight to his chest. "You remember what Mom said and call us. You should put a chair against the door at night."

"Daddy! I promise I will be careful and call twice a week at least. I'll call even more if he teases me." She stood in front of Tucker and looked over her shoulder at him.

"The van and car won't unload themselves," Tucker said. "He opened the back of the minivan and shook his head. "Carrie, did you bring everything you own?"

"Hush, Tuck. Those are essentials for college."

He held up two stuffed animals. "Really?"

She grabbed them and stuck out her tongue.

After getting Caralyn settled, everyone ventured out for lunch.

"I don't have a roommate this semester," Caralyn said. "That's quite a coincidence, Daddy."

He shrugged. "I might have talked to a friend in Housing."

"You should thank your friend for finding our apartment," Tucker said.

After Mom and Dad drove away, Tucker told Caralyn, "Come on. I want to show you around campus."

"I have a map, Tucker. I do know how to read."

"I know, but I need to make sure you don't get lost, Carrie."

"Maybe you should stop calling me that since we're both adults now."

"Yeah, whatever." He drove her around campus and showed her the buildings where she would be having classes. "Let's see if Derren and Richard are here. They are supposed to be arriving today." They headed to the apartment and saw Richard moving in.

"Hi, Richard," Caralyn waved.

He turned around and smiled. "Caralyn, it's good to see you. How was your summer? Did you keep busy?"

"We worked on the farm a lot, but we zipped down to Tennessee for a vacation. How have you been?"

"I worked all summer so I didn't get a chance to go on vacation, but I earned enough to pay for this entire year."

Caralyn remembered how Richard thought she and Tucker were brother and sister, and how he tried to get her to go out with him. *Are you still going to ask me out? I won't sleep with you like the girls Tucker told me about.*

Derren arrived later and Tucker and Richard helped him unload his car.

"How are you guys going to share one bathroom?" Caralyn asked. "And what about the bedrooms? There's only two, and one of them only has one bed."

"We decided to let Richard use the smaller bedroom," Tucker said.

Caralyn stared at him. "I get it. He has girls spend the night, so he needs the privacy."

"Three girls sharing one bathroom might be a problem, but I think guys can adjust without any trouble," Derren said.

"My classes start later in the morning, so I don't need to get up as early as Derren and Tucker," Richard said.

Caralyn walked up to the rectangular dining table. "Are you going to eat here?"

Tucker shook his head. "We will eat on the couch. Why?"

"This table would make a great place to study. You do study occasionally, right?"

"I tried it once," Tucker replied. "Didn't care for it."

"No wonder you're such a twerp. Did you plan to use the couch to separate the living room from the table?"

Tucker shrugged. "No, but it kinda works, huh?"

"Where did you get the TV?"

"It belonged to the previous tenants. They didn't want it, so we offered twenty bucks and they took it."

"Does it work?" She stood in front of it.

"Would we buy it if it didn't?"

She rolled her eyes.

"It works, Carrie, and our stereo gear fits in the cabinet."

She plopped onto the couch. "I'm glad you have an apartment. I can crash here whenever I want."

"Yeah, that ain't gonna happen," Tucker said.

"We will see about that, Tucker McKay. Mom said you have to look out for me."

Tucker shook a finger. "No way, Caralyn. You can't have it both ways. You complain about being too grown up..."

"Don't you want to see me, Tuck?" she asked pressing her fingers to her lips.

He sighed and walked away.

Caralyn spent Saturday with Tucker and Derren. They checked out the football game and ordered pizza. Caralyn ended up spending the night on the couch. Tucker covered her with a blanket, took her shoes off and kissed her cheek.

She woke up when Derren sat on top of her.

"This couch is sure lumpy all of a sudden. It didn't feel this bad last night."

"Get off of me, you moron!" she hollered.

Derren and Tucker laughed as Caralyn struggled to push Derren off the couch. Richard and his new friend Bethany wandered into the room to see what was causing the commotion.

"What's the matter with her?" Richard asked.

"Richard, will you tell Derren to let me up so I can clobber him?"

"That doesn't sound like a smart thing for me to do, Cara."

"Listen, bucko. When I get up I am going to clobber you, too. Get off of me, Derren! You're hurting my legs."

Derren thought he was really hurting her so he moved.

She sat up and punched his arm. "You weren't really hurting me."

"You're a stinker." He grabbed her and pushed her onto her back. He flipped her over and sat on top of her. "This feels better, but there isn't much padding."

"That's because I don't have a big fat butt like you."

"Did you guys hear that? She accused me of having a big butt. I think I should tickle her." Derren began to tickle her ribs.

"Tuck! Make him stop. I mean it."

Derren stopped and let Caralyn get up.

She smacked his knee. "You are such a cretin."

"Sorry, Cara. I thought you were joking."

She ran into the bathroom and came back in a couple of minutes. She jumped on Derren from the back of the couch, but her plan backfired, and she ended up in his lap. He held onto her and wouldn't release her.

"Are you going to behave now, Cara, or do I have to tickle you some more?"

She smiled, and he knew she wanted him to tickle her again. She squealed as Derren tickled her ribs.

Bethany whispered to Richard, "It looks like foreplay to me. Are they a couple?"

Tucker said, "Will you stop, or at least use the bedroom?"

Caralyn looked at Tucker and pointed at Derren. "He started it. He woke me up by sitting on top of me. I'm innocent."

"You were the one who jumped on top of him and started it up again so don't look for sympathy from us."

Caralyn was now on her back on the couch with Derren leaning over her. To Bethany it looked like Derren was ready to kiss her. Neither Richard nor Tucker did anything to help Caralyn.

Tucker winked as he told Richard, "Come on. Let's get something to eat and let the lovebirds enjoy their privacy."

"She looks awfully young. How old is she?" Bethany asked.

"She's fourteen."

Bethany gave Derren a dirty look and whispered to Richard, "He should be locked up for molesting a child."

"It's even worse," Richard said.

"Why?"

"They're cousins."

Chapter Twenty-One

Several days later Caralyn and Bethany bumped into each other outside the dining hall.

"Do you go to school here?" Bethany asked. "I thought you were in high school."

Caralyn recognized her as Richard's 'girlfriend of the week' and answered, "It's my first year here."

"How old are you?"

"I'm sixteen, but I'll be seventeen at the end of November."

"Seriously? How can you be in college?"

"It's a long story," Caralyn said with a sigh.

"I guess Richard was kidding when he said you were fourteen, and I fell for his joke. People do that to me all the time. Is Derren your boyfriend?"

"Derren? No. He's my cousin. Why?"

"I thought you and Derren were lovers when I saw you, and Richard told me you were only fourteen. I knew you weren't fourteen, but you look younger than most students. Most first-year students are eighteen or nineteen. I'm confused though. Richard told me Derren and Tucker are cousins and you and Derren are cousins." Bethany rolled her eyes. "Duh! I'm such an idiot! You are Tucker's little sister. You must think I'm a dumb blonde for real."

Caralyn understood Bethany's faulty reasoning and smiled. "I love Derren dearly, but not as a lover. Tucker and I are..."

"My name is Bethany, by the way. I guess we were never introduced."

"I'm Caralyn. Nice to meet you, Bethany." Caralyn shook her hand. "My older sister is named Beth. Do you go by Bethany or do people call you Beth?"

"My Dad calls me Beth, but no one else really does."

Caralyn and Bethany became friends even though Richard and Bethany broke up. Caralyn eventually got a chance to explain her relationship to Tucker, but it confused Bethany even more, so Caralyn shrugged and dropped the subject.

Caralyn learned how to find her way around campus, made new friends and developed a routine. She wore jeans exclusively, and when she crashed at the boys' apartment, she usually slipped into one of Tucker's or Derren's sweatshirts. Tucker and Derren grew accustomed to her hanging around and treated her like a tomboy. She played football with the guys on the weekends and teased Richard about his womanizing.

"I am so much better at football than you." She tossed the football at him after scoring a touchdown. "You would get better if you didn't try to sleep with every girl you meet."

"Next time I will tackle you and not worry about where I touch you," he replied.

"You'll have to catch me first."

She hung out at Bethany's dorm one day and worked up the courage to ask, "How did you and Richard meet?"

"He saw me coming out of the dorm one day and started talking to me. He was so good looking and charming. I simply had to sleep with him. Have you ever felt that way about anyone, Cara? Oh, silly me! Of course you haven't. You are too young to be thinking about boys. One day you will though."

Caralyn thought about Tucker, but didn't say anything to Bethany about him since she wasn't sure Bethany understood she was not his sister.

One weekend three different guys from her floor asked Caralyn for a date. She politely refused and explained she didn't have time to be dating. She told Tucker about the offers.

"I don't mind if you date as friends, but you need to be careful."

"I'm not that naïve, Tuck. I know these guys would try to get me in bed. I see girls and guys shacking up all the time. Especially the freshman girls. A lot of them jump into bed with guys every weekend."

"They are breaking away from the influence of their parents and trying to grow up real fast."

131

"Duh!" Caralyn sighed. "One of the guys in my nine o'clock lit class asked me to a frat party yesterday. He told me there would be plenty of free beer and a cool band playing. I told him I was busy, but maybe I would another time."

"You should stay away from those parties, Cara. They really prey on freshman girls."

"I don't plan on going to a frat party anytime soon. I'm happy to spend my free time with you guys. Oh, who was that girl that stayed with Richard last weekend? Is she a new one?"

"Yeah, I don't remember her name, and Richard probably doesn't either."

They laughed because it was probably true.

"Do you remember Bethany? She was one of Richard's girls."

"I remember her. I know you guys are friends."

"I'm still not positive she understands you're not my brother."

"She is a blonde, Cara."

Caralyn tucked a lock of hair behind her ear. "So am I! Does that mean you think I am ditzy too?"

"Of course I do, but I love you anyway. Derren is going home this weekend. We should go home so Mom and Dad can see you."

"Okay, I don't have much studying to do this weekend, just some reading, and I can do that on the way home."

"Tell me everything about your week, honey. How are your classes?" Mom hugged her until Caralyn couldn't breath. "Are you eating properly? You look like you've lost weight."

"She's just lost some baby fat, Mom. That's all," Tucker teased Caralyn.

"She does look thinner in the face," Mom said.

Caralyn frowned at Tucker, but knew he was right in a way. She had lost a few pounds.

"Classes are going fine, and I am used to the campus now. I usually meet Tuck and Derren, or sometimes Richard, for lunch and we all try to eat dinner together a couple of times a week. I've been crashing at the apartment on the weekends because the dorm is...” Caralyn hesitated because she didn't want to tell Mom about all the parties and shacking up that happened in the dorm. “The dorm is so boring.”

“Although it's been a long time ago, honey, I do remember what life in the dorm was like,” Mom said.

“It's worse now with boys and girls living on the same floor.”

“Where do you sleep at the apartment, honey?” Mom asked hesitantly.

“I use the living room couch. It's all right. Tucker gives me a blanket and one of his pillows. Don't worry, Mom. Tucker isn't treating me like a sister,” she said sarcastically. “He treats me like one of the guys.”

“That's probably a good idea,” Mom said with relief. “What about their friend?”

“If you mean Richard, he flirts with all the girls, including me.”

“Caralyn!”

She shrugged. “He's not going to do anything. I want to take more of my old jeans back with me. I feel more comfortable in jeans and an old sweatshirt. I guess I am still a tomboy. I haven't worn a dress since I've been on campus. I should bring them all home.”

“I'm happy to hear that, honey. I worry about you with all those older boys around.”

“Mom! You don't need to worry. I'm not going to jump in the sack and mess with any of those guys just to be doing it.”

“I should certainly hope not, Caralyn Ann.”

Chapter Twenty-Two

Caralyn promised to come home to see Mom and Dad once a month. She adjusted to being on her own but still got homesick at times. After one trip home she brought a couple of her favorite stuffed animals back to her dorm room. Derren and Richard saw them on her dresser and teased her.

"Don't make fun of me, Derry. I like to keep them with me."

Richard asked, "Do you sleep with them, Caralyn?"

"Sometimes I do, if you must know," Caralyn answered quietly.

"We're sorry, Cara. We shouldn't be teasing you so much. Come on. Let's eat."

As they were leaving Richard asked Derren, "Why does she act like a little girl at times and other times she is so mature and grown up? It's got nothing to do with how smart she is."

"She is only sixteen. She is still partly a child, even though she would never admit it."

"Do you think she and Tucker have something going on?" Richard asked.

"Why? What do you know?"

"They seem different in a way. A few days ago I swear they were kissing right before I walked into the room."

Derren shrugged. "If they do, that is their business, and if they want it to be a secret, then we shouldn't pry." Derren knew Caralyn and Tucker were in love, and it was only a matter of time until they opened up about it.

Caralyn reached the point where she wanted Tucker to make love to her and didn't care what Derren or Richard might think.

"Why can't you spend the night in my room, Tuck? I see lots of students doing it on my floor, and it's probably like that all over the dorm. I might be the only girl who doesn't let her boyfriend spend the night."

"You are special, and I don't want them to think of you as merely another girl screwing her boyfriend. You are more important to me than a quickie in your room. Besides if I spend the night in your room, Derren and Richard will know why. I don't want them to know if anything happens."

"I guess I don't either, Tuck, but I don't want to wait much longer. I am the only virgin on my floor and maybe the only one in the whole dorm. In fact I might be the only virgin in the whole school!"

"I doubt that very much, Carrie. That girl over there is probably a virgin and those two really fat girls might be. I mean who would want to sleep with them."

"That is so mean, Tuck. You should be ashamed of yourself." Caralyn began to laugh.

"What are you laughing about?"

"I had a vision of the fat girls on top of this really short skinny kid from the dorm."

"You're so bad. I know for certain there is one other virgin in school, Cara."

"Who?"

"Me! Have you forgotten I have never slept with anyone either. Maybe after your birthday we can find a way to be alone."

Caralyn threw her backpack on the table, jumped over the couch and stretched out. "I am beat."

Richard tilted his head while sitting in the recliner. "Do I know you?"

"Hush! Where are Tuck and Derry?"

"Basketball. Road trip. Eastern Indiana University. Any of those ring a bell?"

"Shoot! I haven't seen either of them since Wednesday. Classes and studying should be eliminated."

"Derren was anxious to see Natalie. It can't be easy to maintain a long-distance relationship."

She snorted and said, "How would you know? You have a unlimited harem of girls willing to share your bed."

135

"I heard you had a few offers, Cara," he said with a smirk.

She tried to kick his shin, but missed. "Did I tell you what one guy did?"

"Probably, but tell me again. I'm captivated by your anecdotes."

"You don't know what it means, but anyway. This guy stopped me and said, 'Hey, do you want to screw?' Just like that. I swear! No hello. No smile. Nothing." She gave a dismissive wave. "I asked him if his line ever worked."

"What was his answer?"

"He's a virgin, so what do you think?"

Derren drove Caralyn home on the weekend of her birthday, but Tucker couldn't go because of a basketball game in Iowa.

Derren dropped her off and asked, "Hey, Cara, how are things going with... uh... with your lit class?" *Shoot! I wanted to ask about her and Tucker. I guess I should respect their privacy.*

"I finished that assignment early."

"That's good. I'll pick you up Sunday afternoon. Happy birthday, Cara!"

"Thanks, Derren. Say hi to everyone for me, and I'll be ready Sunday afternoon. Three o'clock okay with you?"

"That's fine. See ya." She waved and watched as he backed out of the driveway. Then she ran into the house. "Mom, Daddy, I'm home! Where is everyone?"

"We're in the utility room, honey. The washer sprang a leak, and there is water everywhere. Be careful."

"Do you need help?"

"Could you grab a couple more towels from the bathroom, please?"

Caralyn helped clean up the mess and neither Mom nor Dad mentioned her birthday. Just before she was about to turn in for the night, Mom remembered.

"Oh, honey, we have been so busy with the mess we almost forgot. Happy birthday, sweetheart."

"Yes, happy birthday, precious," Dad gave her a big hug. "We're sorry we almost forgot."

"It's all right, Daddy. I'm not a baby anymore. Soon I will stop counting my birthdays."

Mom kissed her cheek and said, "I will make you a special dinner tomorrow night. You can invite Nancy. She has been asking about you."

Caralyn sauntered to The Curve the next day to see Nancy.

"Hi, Cara. Can I get you something?"

Caralyn glanced at the menu for only a second. "Could I order the burger basket with everything? How late are you working? I want to invite you for dinner tonight."

"I'm finished at four, so that's enough time to run home and change before I come over. You have to tell me all about college and everything."

A few hours later Nancy and Caralyn were in her bedroom talking about college and catching up on the latest news.

"My dorm room is all right and since I don't have a roommate, there's plenty of room. Tucker and Derren share a two-bedroom apartment with their friend Richard, and I spend a lot of time hanging out with them." She didn't tell Nancy about the changes in her relationship with Tucker. "Are you going out with anyone, Nancy?"

"I've been seeing Terry Mullen from Butler. He goes to Kilkenny Junior College and to our church. It's nothing serious, but he is really sweet. Have you been on many dates since you got to school?"

"Not a single one! I've been too busy to go out with anyone. Please don't say anything to Mom, but the guys in the dorm are only after sex, so I'm not interested in them."

"What about the guy who lives with Tucker?" Nancy asked. "Is he the one who came home with them last year?"

"Oh, that's right you did meet him."

"I did and he's cute, Caralyn, and he seemed interested in you."

"He is really good looking, but he is quite the player if you know what I mean. He has a new girlfriend every week. He and I are friends, but nothing more. It's funny, but he thought Tucker was my brother for the longest time."

"That's not so strange, Cara. Lots of people think you are brother and sister."

"I suppose so. I forget not everyone knows the whole story. Are you still planning to attend Southern with Sandy next year?"

"I'm not sure now. I might start at Kilkenny for the first two years unless I get a scholarship."

"Oh, I hope you don't have to go there. Part of the fun of college is living on campus and the social life. Maybe you will get a scholarship."

"It would be good to get away from home. Sandy really likes it there."

Mom hollered from the kitchen, "Caralyn, dinner is ready!"

"We'll be right there, Mom. Come on, Nancy. Mom made chicken enchiladas, and they are really good!"

During dinner Caralyn and Nancy talked nonstop about school with Mom and Dad McKay.

"Thank you for dinner, Mrs. McKay. The enchiladas were delicious."

"You're welcome, dear. Please have your mother call me soon, and I'll pass along the recipe."

The girls retreated to Caralyn's bedroom again.

"Are there as many boys on your floor as girls?"

"There are more boys than girls. That makes the guys desperate because it is so much easier if you can find a girlfriend who lives on the same floor."

"Do the girls spend the night in the boys' rooms?"

"Sometimes, but not always. There isn't as much sex as people might think. Not all girls are so eager to find boyfriends."

Nancy looked at Caralyn. "Have you been with anyone?"

"No! I'm not interested in those boys. I'm much too busy." Caralyn kept it to herself that there was only one boy who held her interest.

138

Chapter Twenty-Three

Sunday afternoon arrived quickly, and Derren picked up Caralyn for the drive back to school.

"How was your weekend? Did you have a good time? Oh, Mom and Dad said to say hi."

She shrugged. "It was good, but Mom and Dad almost forgot my birthday."

"Oh! That's right you had a birthday. What are you fifteen now?"

"Very funny, Derry. You know exactly how old I am."

"I know and I got you something." Derren handed her a gift.

Caralyn was excited because he had never bought her a birthday present since they were little kids. She shook the package. "What is it?"

"Open it and you'll see."

She opened the gift and couldn't speak at first.

"Derry, where on earth did you find this? It's exactly like my teddy. They don't make them anymore. It's in the original box and in perfect condition."

"I found it at an auction this past summer, and I thought it was the same as yours, so I bought it for you in case you ever need another one."

"That is so sweet of you. Thank you, Derren." She leaned over and kissed him on the cheek.

"I know we tease you a lot about your stuffed animals, but we don't really mean it."

"I know you don't mean anything. I simply can't bear the thought of getting rid of them." They both laughed at her inadvertent pun.

Derren looked at Caralyn and smiled. *Tucker, you are so lucky if you are more than friends with Cara.*

Neither one said anything for a few minutes.

"Did you miss Tucker this weekend, Cara?" He asked to break the momentary silence.

"I didn't miss him because I knew he would be in Iowa for a game. Why are you asking, Derry?" *Do you know about us?*

"Oh, no reason. Just wondered if you would miss him since it was your birthday."

Tucker made it back before Derren and Caralyn. She charged into the apartment to show him her gift.

"Tuck, look what Derren found. It's exactly the same as my bear and still in the box. He found it at an auction last summer. That was so sweet of him."

Tucker wanted to hug her and kiss her, but couldn't because Derren and Richard were in the room. She wanted to kiss him just as much.

"Derren told me about the bear after he found it. I suggested he save it for your birthday, and he agreed."

Derren tried to keep Tucker from saying more but couldn't.

"He was lucky to be able to get it because he had to bid against a collector."

"Precisely how much did you pay for the bear, Derren?" Caralyn put her hands on her hips and looked up at him.

Derren didn't say anything, but Tucker did. "He paid two hundred dollars, Carrie."

"What? You paid that much for a teddy bear for me. The same teddy bear you guys tease me about all the time. You weren't ever going to tell me how much you paid, were you?" Caralyn broke down in tears because of Derren's thoughtfulness.

"It doesn't matter, Cara."

Caralyn wrapped her arms around his neck and hugged Derren tightly and then kissed his cheek. "I will keep him in the box, and maybe someday you will have a little girl, and I will give him to her."

"What if I never have kids?" Derren asked.

"You might, and if not I'll give it to Tucker's baby."

"I didn't know I was expecting," Tucker said with mock surprise.

"Are you ready to head back to your dorm, Caralyn? I'll walk you home," Tucker offered. "It's dark out already."

"I'm ready," Caralyn answered.

Richard said, "I need to see a friend. I'll walk with you guys."

Derren suspected Tucker and Caralyn wanted time alone. "Richard, you promised to read my paper before I turn it in. I really need to finish it before I hit the sack. And you know how to critique the subject better than anyone."

What the hell are you talking about? Richard looked blankly at Derren but then caught on. "Right! I almost forgot. Can you show it to me now?"

Derren and Richard stole into the bedroom as Tucker and Caralyn were getting ready to leave.

"Give me a minute, Carrie. I need to use the bathroom," Tucker told her.

In the bedroom Richard asked Derren, "What is going on?"

"Sorry to make up that story, but I think Tucker and Cara are wanting time to be together without us around."

"Why? They can be alone whenever they want. She is here all the time." Finally it dawned on Richard. "Are you telling me they really have something going on?"

"I'm not positive, but I think so. I saw them kissing, and it wasn't the way you would kiss a sister."

"Unreal!" Richard was astounded. "Well, she isn't his sister, so good for them, I think. Are you sure? It's kinda weird."

Derren and Richard returned to the living room precisely as Tucker came out of the bathroom.

"Are you ready, Tucker? Oh! I need to get my suitcase out of your car, Derren."

"Your laundry too, Cara," Derren reminded her. "You won't have any clean underwear if you forget your laundry."

Caralyn blushed a little as she replied, "I can't go to class without any underwear."

Richard looked at her as she smiled at the guys. He wondered if she and Tucker were already lovers.

"I'll drive you home, Cara. It will be easier than carrying your stuff from here. Tuck can go with me and help carry your laundry upstairs."

Derren parked the car in front of Caralyn's dorm, and the guys unloaded it and carried her stuff inside. They waited for the elevator and Derren remembered, "I need to move the car. I'll be right back."

He ran out to move the car before he got a ticket while Tucker and Caralyn loaded her stuff in the elevator. Now she finally had a chance to kiss him. They held each other close as they kissed.

"I'm sorry I wasn't here for your birthday. I missed you so much."

"I missed you more, and Mom and Dad almost forgot my birthday."

The elevator arrived at her floor, and they carried her laundry to her room as she explained the laundry mishap. Inside her room they kissed and hugged each other again.

"Carrie, I should go."

"Why? I want you to stay. I want you to stay all night."

"I can't, Carrie. If I stay up here too long, Derren might begin to think there's something going on."

"I don't care anymore. I want you to stay with me. I don't want to wait any longer."

"I know, but we need to be patient. I don't have any protection with me, and we can't take a chance. It would be too risky. I need to get back downstairs before Derren comes up here."

They kissed once more and Tucker left.

He saw Derren downstairs.

"I didn't know if you were going to walk home or not."

"I'll take a ride, Derren. Thanks for waiting."

Although it only took five minutes to walk to the apartment from her dorm, Tucker rode with Derren.

"How was the game?"

"Close, but we won by five. They kept fouling me at the end, but I made all my free throws, so we held on."

Derren thought about asking Tucker about Caralyn, but decided against it. He tried to think of a way to let Tucker and Caralyn experience a weekend alone. He snapped his fingers and said, "I've got it!"

"Hey, Richard, how would you like to take a trip to Chicago this weekend?" Derren asked Wednesday morning.

"Yeah, I need to run home to see my parents. They have been after me to visit. We could take the train downtown, and I'll show you around."

Thursday night Derren let Tucker know he and Richard were going to Chicago.

"Would you or Caralyn like to come with us? We could see Chicago together." Derren knew Tucker couldn't go because they had a game Saturday, but he didn't want Tucker to be suspicious and think they were leaving them alone on purpose.

"I can't, Derren. We're playing Wisconsin State Saturday."

"That's right. I forgot. Do you think Cara would want to? I'll ask her later." When Derren saw Caralyn he told her about the trip.

"I would like to, but I don't want to miss the game."

"That's all right, Cara. Maybe another time."

Derren and Caralyn pretended to be disappointed she couldn't go to Chicago, but inside they were both excited. Derren, because his plan worked, and Caralyn because she and Tucker would have time in the apartment without Richard or Derren there.

Chapter Twenty-Four

Tucker called Caralyn and delivered bad news. "Carrie, change of plan. The guys delayed their trip by a day so Richard could finish a paper."

"Oh, Tuck! Why? I was looking forward to tonight so much."

"I know, Carrie. Now we need to wait until Saturday."

"We will only have one night together. I was hoping we would have more time."

The guys woke up early Saturday morning. Derren and Richard left for Chicago and Tucker left to get ready for the game. He wouldn't see Caralyn until the game started. He found it difficult to focus on the game until the team ran out onto the floor of Trout Auditorium. He scanned the crowd for Caralyn and found her in the usual spot. He smiled and waved. She blew him a kiss. Midwest Central blew the game open at the start of the second half and Tucker led the team in scoring again, as usual. He got a loud ovation when he came out of the game with about thirty seconds left. Caralyn waited for him after the game. They held hands as they walked to his car. Once inside the car Caralyn kissed him.

"You played great, Tuck. Could you hear the crowd screaming after you stole the ball that time and sprinted for a slam dunk. I thought the roof would blow off. It was so loud."

"Yeah, I heard the noise. When the crowd gets into the game, it gives us more energy. Are you hungry? I'm starving. Let's get some dinner."

"I'm hungry, but I'm not sure I can eat anything."

"Why not?"

"I'm getting nervous about tonight, Tuck."

"We don't have to do anything if you aren't ready, Carrie. We can do what we have in the past if you want."

"I will be all right, Tuck. Let's eat and then head back to the apartment."

Tucker suggested his favorite place for dinner. He needed a steak and potatoes.

"If we are going there can we stop by my dorm first?"

"Sure, Cara. Do you need to get something?" Tucker stopped in front of her dorm and let her out.

"You should park and wait for me in the lobby, Tuck. I'll run upstairs and come down to meet you. I'll only be a few minutes." She dashed inside and waited for an elevator. Her heart beat a mile a minute as she rushed to change her outfit. She pulled the baby blue, knee-length chiffon dress out of the closet. After checking herself in the mirror, she hustled to the elevator and whizzed downstairs to find Tucker. He was sitting in a chair watching a replay of the game with several students in the lobby. He didn't see Caralyn until she touched his shoulder.

"I'm ready, Tuck." She set her coat on the back of the chair and smiled at him.

He took her hand, and, as he got up and turned to see her, his heart nearly stopped. "Caralyn, you look beautiful." He was stunned by how pretty she looked. "I didn't know you were going to wear a dress."

"Do you like it? I bought it for you." She twirled in a circle to let him see the dress.

"You look amazing, Carrie."

Trent Cussler, who lived across the hall, whistled and said, "Wow! Caralyn, you look great."

"Thank you, Trent."

Tucker helped her with her coat, and adjusted the collar. She held his hand as they walked to the car. Tucker kept stealing glances at her.

"What are you thinking, Tuck?"

"That you're the most beautiful girl on campus."

"Get serious," she said.

When they arrived at the restaurant, the hostess recognized Tucker and seated them right away.

"I guess sometimes it pays to be recognized by people. We would wait for a half hour otherwise."

Tucker ordered his favorite steak and inhaled it. Caralyn ate most of her salmon.

"Are you still nervous, Carrie?"

"A little bit, Tuck, but I will be fine. Can we take this home? I will probably be hungry later."

He touched the tip of her nose. "We can take it home."

Caralyn smiled at Tucker and relaxed. She knew he would make this night unforgettable.

As they left the restaurant, two men stopped Tucker to congratulate him on the game. He was growing accustomed to being recognized and more comfortable talking to strangers. Caralyn waited patiently and beamed with pride as Tucker talked to the fans.

"You are famous, Tuck. Can I have your autograph?" she teased.

"I still don't see why anyone would want my autograph."

In a few minutes they arrived at the apartment.

"Crap!" She exclaimed as they removed their shoes.

Tucker hung their coats in the closet. "What's wrong, Carrie? Did you see Richard or Derren?"

"No, but I just realized I didn't bring anything to wear tomorrow."

"You've got a toothbrush and deodorant here."

"Yeah, but clean underwear would be nice. It's okay." She looked up at him, "Are we really alone, Tuck? I'm afraid Derren and Richard will come home at any moment."

"They won't be home tonight, Carrie. We have the place to ourselves until tomorrow evening. We can do whatever you want, and nothing you don't want."

"Are you as nervous about this as me?"

"How nervous are you?"

"I want to do more than lay on the bed together. That just makes me horny."

"I want to make this night memorable for you, Carrie."

She giggled and then said, "I think I will remember losing my virginity, Tuck."

"What?! I thought we were just going to make out and maybe go a little farther than before."

"Are you forgetting your promise?" she asked.

"What promise?" He scratched his ear then remembered. "You aren't going to hold me to that crazy pact we made ages ago, are you?"

"It's not crazy, and that's exactly what I thought we were going to do." She saw his grin. "You're teasing me."

"Carrie! I've heard stories of girls who lost their virginity in the backseats of cars in a frenzy of sexual fervor that only lasted a minute. I don't want our first experiences to be like that. I've waited this long, and if you change your mind, I will wait even longer for you."

"You're so special," she said. "And I mean that in the best way. Frenzy of sexual fervor, huh? I should write that down."

He looked quizzically at her. "Huh?"

"Never mind. Thank you for being so good to me, Tuck." She slid her arms around his waist and pulled him toward her. "It is still early. What do you want to do?"

"We could watch a movie or see what's on TV. I assume you aren't ready for bed yet."

"I'm not sleepy if that's what you mean." She smiled seductively at him.

"Let's sit on the couch and see what's on TV."

She sat close to Tucker as he flipped through the channels and found a ballgame. As they watched, she snuggled close and toyed with the buttons on his shirt. He moved his hand to her thigh and then her breast. After a few minutes of kissing and touching she whispered, "Tuck, I think I'm ready."

"I'm ready, too, Carrie." He jumped up and held up one finger. "Give me two minutes. Don't move."

"Where are you going? What are you doing?"

"Getting the room ready."

"Did you leave dirty clothes all over the room?"

"No, but I got to do something. Be patient. This won't take long."

He finished, checked the room and turned off the lights.

"What were you doing?" she asked when he returned.

"You'll see." He picked her up and carried her toward the bedroom.

"Will you go slow, Tuck? I want this to last."

"So do I, Carrie. I will go as slow as I can."

"You did bring a condom, right?"

He nodded. "I borrowed one from Richard's stash."

"Borrowed? Can you give it back?"

"Oh, I guess I stole it because I can't return it. I hope it fits. I couldn't exactly try it on."

"It better."

"I won't know until we... you know."

"I want you to undress me slowly and kiss me all over."

They got to the doorway and he tried to squeeze through.

"Tuck! You bumped my head."

"Sorry, Carrie. Let me try again."

This time he bumped her feet into the door frame.

"Tucker! What are you doing? Put me down before you knock me out."

"I got it this time." He turned and slipped into the bedroom.

"Don't be in a rush," she said as he set her down. "Oh, Bubby! You bought candles. How romantic."

"I thought it was a nice touch. I hope the room doesn't catch on fire."

Tucker followed her instructions. He removed her dress and hung it up in the closet. He kissed her mouth and then her neck and then her chest. He kissed her belly and made raspberry noises on her belly button.

"Stop that, Tuck. It tickles."

"I used to do that when we were kids."

"We aren't kids anymore," she whispered.

He unhooked her bra and removed it easily.

She giggled and said, "You removed it like an expert."

"It was easier the second time."

"Kiss me there, Tuck."

He kissed her breasts and teased them with his tongue.

"That feels good." She looked at the candles and smiled. "You remembered them."

She undid his shirt and removed it and then pulled his t-shirt over his head. She rubbed her hands over his muscled chest and kissed him.

"Your chest wasn't always this hairy."

"You didn't have breasts either," he said with a grin.

"You better be serious, or else I will go home."

She unbuckled and unzipped his jeans and they fell to the floor. He stepped out of them and kicked them aside. They were quiet except for some passionate breathing and purring-like sounds from Caralyn. Tucker put his hands on her hips and slipped them down to her pale blue cotton panties. Slowly he tugged them down. He kissed her tenderly still holding onto her panties. He slipped them to her knees and then to the floor. He lifted one foot and then the other to remove them and then set them on the dresser by her bra.

She looked at the smiley face on his boxers and snickered. "You won't be needing these any more tonight." She tugged them down. He stepped out of them. She picked them up and flung them across the room then giggled.

"What?" he asked putting a hand over his privates.

She pointed at his feet. "You're still wearing your white socks. It's funny."

"Sorry." He removed his socks and tossed them aside. He took her in his arms and carried her to the bed.

"I can smell blueberries," Caralyn mentioned softly.

He pointed to the candles on the left. "Those are blueberry scented and others are apple cinnamon. They didn't have strawberry. Do you like them?"

"Yes, they make the room smell fresh and remind me of the kitchen at home."

"I didn't want anything too overpowering."

"They are perfect," Caralyn said. "Don't put your thing on yet, Tuck. I want to kiss and cuddle first."

149

Tucker slipped into bed next to her. They kissed, held each other close and used their hands to explore. He took his time as he kissed her.

"Now, Tuck. I am ready. I can't wait any longer."

Tucker sat on the edge of the bed and opened the package.

"Hurry, Tuck," she urged.

"Don't rush me, Carrie. I'm not exactly an expert at this."

"Why didn't you practice putting one on?" She sat up and looked around him.

"I didn't think about it. Now there's a lot of pressure."

"Just pretend you are shooting a free throw."

He looked over his shoulder. "That's not helping, Cara."

"Sorry, Tuck." She moved onto her back. "I will wait."

He slipped on the condom and moved into position. "If it hurts too much, I will stop, Carrie. I don't want to hurt you."

"Beth told me the pain is only for a little time if at all."

"I love you, Carrie." He gazed into her eyes. The candles provided just enough light for them to see each other.

"I love you too, Tuck." She helped guide him to the right spot. He entered her slowly. She winced for a second.

He froze. "Should I stop, Carrie?"

"No! Don't stop whatever you do." The momentary pain she expected to give way to extreme pleasure didn't happen. She winced again.

"I'm going to stop, Carrie." He pulled out and lifted up. "We can kiss and..."

"No! Put it back. You were in the wrong spot."

"Carrie, I didn't know I needed a road map."

"Shut up." She moved him a little. "Try it now. Go slow!"

He tried again and she winced. "That's it. I'm not doing this if it's going to hurt you."

"No, Tuck." She grabbed his shoulders. "It's starting to feel better. Beth told me I would love how it felt."

Tucker grinned. "I kinda like it."

"You're a guy. You're supposed to like it. Lift up a little."

"Why?"

"Because your hip is crushing mine."

He lifted up but his knee bumped against her thigh.

"Ow! Stop it. Are you being clumsy on purpose?"

"No! It's not like basketball. I've been playing basketball all my life."

"Please don't start talking about today's game."

"I won't." He shifted again. "Is that better?"

"I think so. That thing won't come off, will it?"

He shrugged. "I don't think so. It's pretty tight."

"I think that's the right place."

"How many places can there be?"

She smacked his arm. "Don't make fun."

"I wasn't."

Ten minutes later they lay side by side.

"Are you okay, Caralyn? Are you sorry we did this? he asked.

She pulled up the sheet and smiled at him. "I'm all right. That felt so good after we got the hang of it. Are we going to do it again? I hope we can."

"We will, Carrie. Just be patient."

"I didn't mean tonight."

"Good because I only borrowed one condom."

"Next time steal more than one," she said.

Chapter Twenty-Five

"Carrie, wake up. We need to get out of bed."

She slowly came awake and smiled at Tucker.

"How are you, Carrie? Are you okay?" He used his elbow to sit up and brushed the hair off her face.

She stretched her arms over her head. "I feel great! What time is it?"

"It's after twelve. We need to get up."

"Did I hear you get up earlier?"

"I got up around eight to take a leak..."

"Gross!"

"Sorry, I guess you didn't need to know that. Anyway, I did my... you know... then I came back to bed. It felt so good to cuddle with you." He pulled back the covers. "Get up, sleepyhead."

She pulled on his arm. "Not yet. We don't need to go anywhere."

He looked at her and tilted his head. "Are you saying what I think you are? We did finally figure it out..."

"Yeah, after you tried to put it in the wrong spot," she teased. "The guys won't be back until later. We are still naked. You love basketball practice. Wouldn't you like to practice making love again?"

"But I used my only condom last night."

She pulled the cover over her chest and rolled her eyes. "Where did you get it?"

He pointed to the other bedroom. "From Richard's drawer."

"Was it the only one?"

"No, he 's got lots of... Oh! I get it."

"Not unless you steal another one."

"Two?"

"Don't push your luck."

"Oh crap! Now we really need to get up." She jumped out of bed and looked at Tucker. She blushed because he was staring at her. "Can I borrow a shirt? Or do you want me to stay naked?"

"Let me think." He smiled at her.

He looked around for his boxers and saw them draped over the light fixture above Derren's headboard. "Nice toss, Cara." He put them on while she watched. He grabbed a shirt from his closet. "Try this."

"It's a dress shirt," she said handing it back. "'Give me a t-shirt or a sweatshirt."

He tossed the dress shirt on the unmade bed, picked out a sweatshirt and handed it to her.

"That's better, Tuck."

He stared as she slipped it over her head then quickly put shorts on over his boxers and grabbed a t-shirt for himself.

"Are you hungry? I could make bacon and eggs if you want."

"That would be fine. I need to use the bathroom. I'll be right back." She returned in a couple of minutes.

"Are you okay, Cara?"

She blushed as she told Tucker, "I'm fine."

They ate breakfast and then Caralyn wanted to shower. "I didn't bring anything to wear today. What should we do?"

"Can you wear what you wore yesterday until we go to your dorm and get clean clothes?"

She fiddled with her earring. "I guess so. It's not like I had them on all that long."

They showered and got ready to walk back to her dorm. In the hallway outside of her room she saw Trent, the guy who whistled at her the night before.

"Hi, Caralyn. Nice dress," Trent said with a wry smile.

She blushed because she knew he suspected she spent the night with Tucker. She and Tucker hurried to her room and she picked out clean clothes to wear.

"Tuck, Trent must know we were together last night. Did you hear what he said about my dress?"

"It's all right if he knows, Cara. We won't be able to keep it a secret forever."

153

Derren and Richard returned home that evening and saw Tucker and Caralyn studying at the table. Caralyn wore her old faded jeans and one of Tucker's sweatshirts over her top. They had cleaned the apartment and made sure there was no trace of the previous night. Caralyn saved all the candles. They had even laundered the bed sheets.

"How was Chicago? Did you guys enjoy your trip?" Tucker asked.

"It was all right. I wish we had more time. There is so much to see. How was the game and the rest of your weekend?" Richard asked. *I always enjoy a weekend without you guys hanging around.*

"We won, and the weekend was okay." Tucker glanced at Caralyn. "We ate dinner at the Texas Roadhouse last night."

Derren looked at Cara and swore she was blushing. He could tell they enjoyed the time alone because she appeared to be glowing. He was pleased his plan had worked but didn't say anything.

"We're studying for classes. Are you guys hungry? We could order pizza or Chinese."

"How about Chinese? Can we order Chinese, Tuck?" Caralyn asked.

"Sure! You can choose whatever you want, Carrie."

She retrieved the menu from the drawer next to the fridge and she and Richard called in an order for delivery. She and Tucker returned to their studying. Derren and Richard unpacked and then Richard joined Derren in his bedroom.

"Do you think they did it?" Richard asked quietly as he looked around the room to see if anything looked different.

Derren looked at him. "Yes, they did, but we can't say anything to them. As long as they are keeping it a secret, we won't let on we know. Okay?"

"Okay with me. They think nobody can tell they are in love. All you need to do is watch how they look at each other. It's so obvious."

"Yeah, but they don't know that."

"Caralyn looks like the happiest girl in the world."

"Yeah, I know. Let's not spoil this time for her."

"I won't say a word to either of them."

The food arrived and the guys removed their study materials from the table at Caralyn's request. She wanted to eat at the table and the guys agreed to do whatever she wanted. She set the table and fussed over the guys. They pretended not to notice and soon finished all the food. After eating they sat and watched TV for a while.

At eleven, Caralyn told Tucker, "I should go home. I'm falling asleep, and I need to get up early."

"I'll drive you home, Cara."

"Can we walk instead?"

Tucker shrugged and said, "Okay, if you want to freeze."

"Good night, guys. See you later," Caralyn told Derren and Richard.

They walked down the stairs and out the front door. Derren moved to the window and watched as they walked along the sidewalk.

"Richard, look at this."

Richard looked out the window and saw Tucker holding her hand as Caralyn skipped along beside him. They stopped for a moment and Caralyn put her arms around his neck. They held each other close and kissed tenderly. Derren closed the curtain and smiled.

Chapter Twenty-Six

A week later Richard and Derren decided to spend the weekend in Stockton Woods. Tucker and Caralyn had the entire weekend alone. They spent Friday night in bed making love and slept until noon on Saturday. Tucker began to wonder why Derren and Richard were both gone.

"Do you think they suspect anything, Cara?"

"I don't think so. Why?"

"No reason. It's weird how they made sure we knew they were going to be gone this weekend."

"Maybe they saw us kissing or something, but I don't think they know about us sleeping together."

"You're probably right. I suppose it doesn't matter."

For the rest of the semester Tucker and Caralyn kept their relationship a secret. At least they thought it was a secret as Derren and Richard pretended not to know about it.

At Christmas break Caralyn and Tucker were back in Stockton Woods. Mom and Dad had two more days of school so Caralyn and Tucker were home alone during the day. They thought about making love, but there were too many interruptions. People called all the time and old friends stopped to see them.

"We will have to wait until tomorrow or maybe tonight, I guess," Tucker said.

"We are definitely going to share a bed sometime before school starts again, Tucker," she insisted.

Mom and Dad returned home. Caralyn helped prepare a honey ham and cheesy potatoes for dinner. Dad and Tucker talked about school and the basketball team in the living room.

"Dinner is ready," Caralyn announced as she sat on the arm of Dad's old brown leather recliner.

"It smells so good, princess."

"Thank you, Daddy," She kissed his cheek and stuck out her tongue at Tucker.

After dinner Caralyn and Tucker took care of the clean-up while Mom and Dad attended a small gathering of friends at the Garnett home.

"Do you want to take a chance and... you know?"

"We can't. Mom said they were only going to be there for an hour or so."

"We can do it in less than an hour, Carrie." Tucker kissed her and put his hands on her hips and drew her close.

"I don't want a quickie! I know you could do it in a couple of minutes, but I want it to be romantic and not rushed. Besides I told Nancy I would call her tonight."

Two hours passed before Mom and Dad returned. Tucker looked at Caralyn and whispered, "See! There was time."

She shrugged and said, "I'm going to get ready for bed, but I want to read for a while."

"We're going to bed. We have school," Mom said.

"Night, Mom. We'll be quiet."

They stayed up and eventually Caralyn fell asleep on the couch with her book in her hands. Tucker carried her to bed and kissed her good night before going to sleep at Grandma's house.

By the time Caralyn woke up the next morning, Mom and Dad had left for school. Caralyn thought about going to Grandma's house to see if Tucker was awake. At precisely that moment the back door opened, and he walked in.

"I was going to see if you were awake. Mom and Dad are gone already."

Without saying a word, Tucker scooped her up in his arms and carried her to her bedroom. He dropped her on the bed.

"We have enough time for more than a quickie now."

"Okay, but Nancy and I are going into Butler to do our Christmas shopping. She's supposed to be here at ten."

Tucker glanced at the clock, barely visible between two stuffed bears, on top of the dresser.

"It's a little after eight. I think there's time before you need to get ready." He grinned as she scooted under the covers.

"Do you have...?"

He reached into his pocket and pulled out his protection.

She squealed. "Oooh! Two of them."

He slipped into bed next to her and they began kissing. A moment later they were undressing each other.

Nancy knocked on the front door at five minutes after ten. Caralyn ran to let her in.

"I'll be ready in a couple minutes," Caralyn said as she hurried back to her bedroom.

Nancy sat on the couch to wait.

"Hey, Nancy, how's things?" Tucker wandered in from the kitchen.

"Everything is going great. I heard you are the leading scorer on the team. That must make you feel good."

They talked until Caralyn returned.

"We'll be back later, Tuck." She grabbed her purse and pulled Nancy out the door

"See ya later, Tuck." Nancy shouted over her shoulder as Caralyn nearly dislocated her arm. "Ow! That hurts, Cara. What is your hurry? I wanted to talk to Tucker about school."

"You can talk to him later if you want."

Caralyn and Nancy spent time shopping and ate lunch, but Caralyn didn't tell Nancy about her relationship with Tucker even though they were close friends.

Mom and Dad returned home in the early afternoon.

"I don't have school until next year," Mom said. "Where's Cara?"

"She and Nancy drove into Butler. I don't know when she's going to get home."

"I am not returning until mid-January," Dad bragged.

"This is for you, Carrie." Tucker reached behind the Christmas tree and handed her a oval box wrapped in shiny red paper.

"But you already bought me three books."

"Yeah, but I found this in the clearance bin at Woolmarks in Butler. It was cheap."

She ripped the paper into shreds and opened the box. She gasped and put her hand to her heart.

"Lucky for me, it was engraved already," Tucker said with a grin.

"What is it, Caralyn?" Dad asked.

"It's a charm bracelet with a heart-shaped charm. It's engraved with our initials." She handed the box to Dad then kissed Tucker on the mouth in front of Mom and Dad.

Dad's mouth opened, and he tried to speak but no words came out. He looked at Mom and pointed. She smiled at him and put a finger to her mouth to keep him quiet.

As Jim and Sarah lay in bed that night she reminded him, "They are not brother and sister even though that's how you think of them. They are in love, and you need to pretend you don't know anything. That shouldn't be too difficult for you."

"I guess so, if that's what you say I should do. When in the world did this happen? Frankly, I am totally confused. I've always thought of Caralyn as my daughter. You don't think they've done more than kiss, do you?"

"I'm certain she's still your innocent little girl."

Caralyn came out to the kitchen in her pajamas and saw Dad sitting in his usual spot at the table. She kissed the top of his head. "Good morning, Daddy. Did you sleep well?"

"I did. How did you sleep, honey?"

"I slept like a baby."

Tucker entered through the back door a few minutes later. "Morning, Mom. Morning, Dad. Hey, Carrie. How's everybody?"

"We are all fine," Mom answered.

"'Bout time you got up lazybones," Caralyn teased Tucker, and he teased her back just like old times.

Dad wondered if Mom was imagining things. *Maybe Caralyn got carried away last night because of Tucker's gift.*

159

Later, as he and Mom did the dishes, he asked, "Are you sure they are in love with each other? They acted the same as always at breakfast. They teased each other and carried on like when they were growing up."

"You can tell by the look in their eyes. Caralyn lights up whenever Tucker is close, and it's obvious Tucker is in love with her."

He scratched his ear. "Are you sure?"

"Trust me, Jim," Sarah smiled.

"Well, it might be complicated since they have grown up together."

"True, but remember Caralyn has known she was adopted for a long time now. She doesn't think of Tucker as a brother anymore. Maybe she never did. Maybe they were always aware of the difference. Who knows?"

"What will people say? There are still people in town who think she is our daughter. We should make her come to Dickinson."

"Almost everyone knows we are her guardians. Maybe it's a good thing we never legally adopted her and changed her name. Everyone in town knows her as Caralyn Dawson, so they must realize she is not Tucker's sister."

Caralyn and Tucker got back and joined Mom and Dad in the kitchen.

"What were you guys talking about?" Caralyn asked.

"We were talking about you, dear. We were talking about how we never legally adopted you and changed your name."

"Was someone asking about me?"

"Actually a new lady at church did ask about you, honey. She assumed you were my daughter and called you Caralyn McKay. Mrs. Boyd corrected her and told her your name was Caralyn Dawson."

Caralyn glanced at Tucker and thought it was a good thing the McKays never formally adopted her, even though she would always think of them as her parents.

160

Chapter Twenty-Seven

"I don't regret what we did, Tucker. I wanted you to be my first, but we are still too young to get married or start a serious relationship. I think we better slow down even though I really like having sex."

"I kinda like it, too," Tucker said.

"Yes, but I feel confused emotionally. Not physically."

"Are you afraid to do it again because you think Derren and Richard will find out and not approve?"

"Maybe a little."

"We could tell them and get it out in the open."

"Not yet, Tuck, please. I will always love you, and I hope we are friends forever—even when we are old. Maybe someday we will get married, but right now our priority is to make it through school. I want to be a writer, and I know you want to play in the NBA. We should be careful and not jeopardize our dreams and goals."

"So do you want to jump in the sack and make love?"

"You better believe I do. I want you so much!" she teased back. She looked at him and her face morphed from a smile to an intensely serious look. "You may not like this suggestion, but I think we need to start seeing other people. I'm not saying that because I don't love you, but if we see other people, no one will learn about our relationship."

He stared into her eyes for a moment. "You feel guilty about what we've done, don't you? Some people might think it's rather incestuous."

"That's a bunch of bull! We aren't related. Derren and I are related. I could never sleep with him."

Tucker understood her feelings, and they continued to be discreet about their relationship. She and Trent talked a few times and she enjoyed his company. She decided to say yes if he asked her for a date again. Tucker started dating Laurie Miller, a girl he met in his business communication class.

"I can date whoever I want, Tucker McKay. You can't tell me how to run my life, and he's from my Wednesday class. His name is Brian Hinsche, so he's not a complete stranger." She and Tucker argued in front of Derren and Richard. She gave Tucker a hard look and turned to leave, but Derren stood in the doorway. "Are you going to tell me how to run my life now too, Derren?"

"Caralyn, Tucker is looking out for you. He isn't trying to run your life."

"Back off, Derren, while I still like you." She pushed him out of the way.

"Fine, Caralyn. Have it your way." Derren looked at Tucker and wondered what had gotten into her.

She stormed away and when she got to her room, she called the guy from her class and accepted a date with him.

Back at the apartment Tucker told Derren, "She is having her monthly PMS. It really upsets her, and that's why she got so mad. I think she will be all right."

Later, Richard asked Derren, "What's going on with those two? Last month there were in love, and now they're fighting and seeing other people."

Derren shrugged. "I don't have a clue, but it's got to be complicated for them."

Richard assumed Tucker and Caralyn ended their brief affair because that's how he terminated his relationships. He would move on after having sex.

Caralyn went on a date with Brian, and afterward he made a pass at her. He succeeded in groping her before she made him stop.

"I will crush your balls if you try that again," she said making fists.

"Come on! I spent money for a movie, and now you won't even let me touch you."

"I'm not a hooker you can buy sex from." She called him a name designed to make him understand she was serious. "Take me home before I start screaming."

Brian took her back to her dorm, and she called Tucker. "I'm sorry I got mad at you. Will you forgive me?"

"Of course I will, Carrie. Are you all right?"

"If you mean is my period done, no. Not yet, but I am better. I went out with Brian tonight, but it didn't go well. He made a pass at me, but I didn't let him complete it. I intercepted the pass and ran it back for a touchdown. Then I called him a name that would get me in trouble if Mom heard it."

Tucker laughed because he could imagine what she called the guy. "Are you sure you are all right, Carrie?"

"I'm okay, Tuck. I'm tired, and I want to go to bed. I wish you were here to keep me company, but I know you can't."

"I'll talk to you in the morning, Carrie. Come on over when you wake up. Sleep well."

Caralyn walked into the apartment the next morning and saw Derren first. "I'm sorry I got mad at you, Derry."

"It's okay. Tucker explained everything."

"I don't know why, but I get so emotional right before my period." She blushed. "Maybe I shouldn't say that to you."

"It's okay. I know you can't help it." He picked her up, hugged her and whispered, "You're still my favorite cousin."

"You're my second most favorite cousin... after Davey."

Tucker came out of his room and saw them hugging. "Hey, what's going on here?"

Derren set her down and Caralyn turned around to see Tucker. She turned back to Derren and kissed him on the mouth, surprising him. "Derren and I are having an affair if you must know. I'm sorry you had to find out like this."

Richard wandered into the room just as Caralyn kissed Derren, dropped his book as he caught what Caralyn said. "You and Derren are having an affair. I thought she was..."

Derren quickly told them, "It's true, Caralyn, and I have been sleeping together and that's where we are going now. We are going to spend the day in bed." He tossed her over his shoulder much to her surprise and carried her to the bedroom.

163

She squealed as he tossed her on his bed. "Derry! What are you doing?"

"Just teasing you, Cara. You can get up now."

"No, I'll stay here in bed with you. Kiss me again."

"I didn't kiss you. You kissed me."

"Didn't you like it?"

Tucker and Richard stood in the doorway watching and listening. They burst into laughter as Caralyn tried to kiss Derren again, but he moved out of the way and she fell out of bed.

"Ow! That hurt."

"Come on. Let's get something to eat," Tucker said. "You can continue your affair later."

Caralyn's first year away at college passed quickly, and it was time to make housing arrangements for next year. She and Bethany talked about becoming roommates, but that fell through when Bethany decided to transfer closer to home. Caralyn arranged for a single room again. She would end up in the same dorm and on the same floor as this year. She scheduled her classes so she and Tucker would have more time together.

"Should we tell them we slept together? I think they already suspect it, Cara."

"No, Tuck! I don't want them to know yet. You and Laurie are going out, and they think she is your girlfriend."

"She's not my girlfriend, Carrie. We go out but just as friends—sorta like you and Trent. Has he ever tried anything?"

"He kissed me, but he's never made a real pass at me."

"He's probably waiting for the right moment."

"So you think he is waiting for the perfect moment to seduce me, huh?" She stood with her hands on her hips and grinned.

"Maybe. Some guys are patient."

"Are you being patient with Laurie like you were with me, Tuck?"

"Cara! You know I wanted our first time to be special and not a spur of the moment decision. Laurie is just a friend."

"I know you kissed her. She is so pretty and better built than me. She looks like a supermodel. She probably doesn't have scars on her knees, or blotchy skin. She knows how to use makeup. She makes me look like a frump."

"Carrie, don't put yourself down. You are just as pretty as Laurie, and she's not tall enough to be a supermodel."

She looked up him. "How tall are you now, anyway? I think you're taller than Derren."

"Coach measured everyone before the season and I was six two, but I might have grown another inch."

"Well, don't grow anymore. I don't want to be a foot shorter than you."

"I'll try, but I don't think it's something I can control."

"Speaking of growing more," Caralyn said with a grin. "Laurie is certainly is more developed than me if you know what I mean. Have you done more than kiss her?"

"I'm not telling you anything else, Caralyn!"

She smiled because he was blushing.

Chapter Twenty-Eight

"Caralyn, Ray and I are going camping in Wisconsin. Would you like to join us? We're going to ride bikes and maybe do a little hiking. You usually come to Chicago in the summer. This would be something different."

"I would, but I don't want to sleep in a tent by myself. Could I bring Nancy?"

"Sure. You could see if Derren and Tucker are busy."

"You wouldn't mind if they come?"

"Why not? You would need to borrow the McKay's van and bring two tents. Didn't Tucker and Nancy date?"

"Yeah, but he's too busy to see her now," Caralyn said. "He's been seeing a different girl at school."

"Ask the McKays and call me back."

"Please, Mom! It would be so much fun. Nancy's father said she could go, and there will be three guys along to keep an eye on us. We will be safe."

"Beth and Ray both drink alcohol. I'm not sure I want you to be tempted if they buy beer for themselves," Dad McKay said. "Did you mention that to Mr. Young?"

She shook her head. "No, but I'm not going to be drinking beer. I don't like it."

"How do you know you don't like it, honey?" Mom asked. "Have you tasted it before?"

"I tried a little bit when I visited Beth in Chicago last year. But that doesn't mean I am going to be drinking it again. It only took two sips for me to realize I didn't like it."

"We will think about it tonight and let you know our decision in the morning. Will that be all right?"

"Yes, Daddy. I will abide by your choice, but I really, really, really want to go!" She raced to her room.

"What do you think, Sarah. Should we let her? I don't like the fact she had a beer. She's too young to try alcohol, but Beth might not see it that way."

"She is growing up. We can't treat her like a child anymore," Sarah said. "She will be eighteen in November and will want to be making her own decisions. We need to trust her to make the correct ones."

"She has already finished a year of college. It seems like it wasn't all that long ago she was still so little." Dad thought about it for a moment and made up his mind. "We need to let her go. I will call Beth and Ray to make it totally clear I don't want Caralyn, or any of the other kids, to be drinking any alcohol."

"Ray and I will look after Caralyn and Nancy and not let them get into any trouble," Beth said. "I think they will have a great time. We've camped at Cornell Lake several times."

"I am relying on you to follow through, Beth."

"I understand. I really don't think she will be interested after what happened the last time," Beth said.

Dad McKay stared at the phone after Beth hung up. "Do I even want to know what happened?"

"Caralyn, we made our decision last night. You can go." Dad informed her a few minutes later.

"Oh, Daddy! Thank you so much. I can't wait. I'm going to call Nancy and tell her we're going."

Dad decided to let Tucker take the minivan on the trip. They would be able to pack more gear in it than Tucker's Civic.

"I will behave, Mom, I promise." Caralyn bounced on her toes as she, Nancy, Tucker and Derren got ready to leave.

"I know you will, but this is the first time you've gone on vacation without us. I'm sad to see you leave. I will miss my little girl."

"Mom! Tucker and Derren will be with me, and I've visited Beth and Ray plenty of times by myself."

"I know, but I will still worry. Promise you will call me every night, okay?"

"I will try, but if we are out of cell phone range, I won't have a chance."

"Try to call as often as you can, honey." She turned to Tucker. "You look after the girls, and be nice to Nancy. She still likes you even though you are too busy to call her."

"I will be nice to Nancy, but I can't guarantee anything about her." He pointed to Caralyn.

Caralyn made a face at him. "We might not even talk to you, dweeb brain."

"Drive safely, son." Dad held out the keys. "I only want you or Derren to drive the van. Cara is not used to it, and I don't want her to drive it through a lot of traffic."

"Daddy!" Caralyn tried to swipe the keys.

Tucker grabbed the keys, laughed and said, "Derren and I will do all the driving, Dad. You don't have to worry about us. We don't want to risk our lives by letting her behind the wheel."

They piled into the already loaded van, drove out of town, merged onto Interstate 57 and headed for Chicago. Two tents and their bicycles took up a lot of room.

"Cara, I only packed four nice tops. Will we have a chance to do laundry?" Nancy asked.

"I didn't pack much underwear, so I sure hope we can."

A couple of hours later Caralyn pounded on the back of the driver's seat. "Tuck, we need to stop. I'm starving, and I have to pee."

"We can stop at the McDonald's close to the exit. We should be there in a few minutes. I don't want to run into New Lebanon. It would take too much time."

"I can wait till then," Caralyn said. "How about you?" she asked Nancy.

"I'm good."

Two and a half hours later Tucker pulled into the Oasis. "I see a van, Tucker." Caralyn pointed. "Beth told me they bought a red minivan. That must be it."

"I see it now."

Derren spotted Ray coming out of the Oasis, "There's Ray. Beth must be inside."

Tucker found a spot close to Beth and Ray's new minivan. Even though their immediate future didn't include children; they bought a minivan for their camping and canoe trips. Ray saw them, waved and walked over.

"You guys made it quick. We weren't expecting you for another half hour. Good to see you." Ray shook hands with them. "Caralyn, you look fantastic. Are you ready for camping in the deep woods with the bears and other creatures."

"Don't even try to scare me, Ray. It won't work. I know we will be staying in a campground. Where's Beth?" she asked then noticed gray hair in his ponytail.

"She's inside. She'll be out in a second," Ray pointed to the building. "She is anxious to see you and hear all about your first year of college. If you want to ride with us, you can. You and Beth can catch up on news."

"Can Nancy ride with?"

Ray smiled at Nancy. "I'm Ray. You're welcome to ride along."

"Thanks, but I'll stay with Tucker and Derren for now."

"I will ride with you for a while," Caralyn said. "Tucker and Derren won't let me listen to the CDs I want to hear."

"You can play whatever music you want as long as it's not rap."

"Thank you, Ray." Caralyn turned to Tucker and Derren and stuck out her tongue. "You can listen to your crappy music."

"Ray, are you sure you want her to ride with you?" Tucker asked. "She can be a real pain in the butt sometimes."

"If we get tired of her, we will toss her out, and you can pick her up along the way."

"Very funny guys," Caralyn answered sarcastically. "There's Beth." Caralyn ran to her sister and gave her a hug. Since they were older, she and Beth got along better.

Four hours later they arrived at the turnoff to Cornell Lake Campground. Caralyn could see a large hill in the distance.

"Look! It's a mountain," she exclaimed.

"The campground is on top. It's mostly woods and covers about ten acres," Beth explained.

"It's not quite a mountain, Cara, but it sure is bigger than anything near Stockton Woods," Ray said.

Tucker followed Ray when he turned onto a gravel road. After checking in at the farm at the bottom of the hill, they began the two mile drive to the top.

"This is the road we will be using to come and go. It will be easy to ride down, but... you know. What goes down must come up," Ray informed Caralyn.

Caralyn swiveled her head as Ray drove slowly up the winding road.

"Beth, where are the showers?"

"There aren't any, Caralyn. We are going to rough it for a few days. The only water up here is there by that little building. There is a shower head on the side of the building but there isn't any hot water. It takes getting used to, but it's better than no shower at all. That's the outhouse there."

"Beth! Are you telling me I have to shower outdoors with only cold water and that crummy looking building is the outhouse?"

"Yeah, sorry, Cara. Are you disappointed?"

"Heck no! It sounds like fun. A real adventure! I think I will shower in my bathing suit though. I don't want to shower naked where everyone can see."

"I think that's the way people do it up here, Cara. I've never seen anyone showering naked there, and Ray and I have stayed here several times. We don't even shower naked here."

"Oh, Beth! We are going to have so much fun."

They chose one of the more isolated campsites for privacy, a good view of the sunset, and the fire ring. It didn't take long to unload the minivans and set up the tents. They parked the minivans in front of their site for even more privacy. Ray and Tucker carried a picnic table to the site. Beth, Caralyn and Nancy stole away for a hike and noticed only one other campsite being used at the time.

170

"Doesn't anyone know about this place?" Caralyn asked.

"Later in the summer, this place will be more crowded," Beth explained. "That's why Ray and I like to come up here now. Plus it's cooler, and we like campfires at night."

They ate a light supper and waited for the sun to set.

"Look at the colors. There's purple and orange and such a vivid red. Don't you love it, Tuck?" Caralyn asked as she sat next to him on the three foot thick trunk of a tree that had been likely hit by lightning and left to lay where it had fallen.

When they were ready to call it a night, Beth joined Caralyn and Nancy, who sat by themselves staring at all the stars in the dark sky.

"Look, Beth. You can see so many stars up here. Way more than back home."

"I see." Beth put her hands on Caralyn's shoulders and asked, "Did you remember to call home?"

"Shoot! I forgot. We got so busy."

"Sometimes you can get cell phone reception up here, but not always."

Caralyn eventually got in touch with Mom and told her about the campground and about the possibility of not being able to call sometimes.

"That's all right, honey. We know the boys will take care of you. I hope you can sleep okay at night. If you get scared, tell Nancy."

"Mom! I won't get scared of the dark."

"I mean if it storms or something. You still get scared during bad storms."

"Not as much as I used to. I'll be all right. I'll try to call you tomorrow night."

"Good night, honey. We love you."

"I love you, too. Good night."

Chapter Twenty-Nine

Ray woke up as soon as it got light and started making breakfast. Soon the other guys were up. Beth came out of the tent wearing a form-hugging white t-shirt walked up to Ray and gave him a long kiss. Tucker and Derren noticed and tried not to stare.

"Are the girls still sleeping, Tucker?" Beth asked.

"I think so," he answered.

"Maybe you should wake them up."

Tucker walked to the tent, and didn't hear anything.

"Carrie! Time to wake up, sleepyhead." He listened but didn't hear them stirring. "Nancy, are you guys awake?" He heard the sleeping bags rustle.

"We're awake, Tucker, but Caralyn needs to get dressed. Don't come in."

"I wasn't planning to." He waited outside until the girls came out.

"Why didn't you let us sleep?" Caralyn came out of the tent looking like a mess. Her long hair was all tangled up. "I need to pee, Tuck. Nancy does, too."

"The outhouse is back that way." Tucker looked at her and noticed she was not wearing a bra under her long t-shirt. He looked at Nancy and saw she was fully dressed. He walked away and decided to help Ray with breakfast.

Derren asked, "Is Sleeping Beauty awake?"

"Yeah, but Nancy had wake to her up."

"I hope she's not grouchy. She can be kinda grumpy if she doesn't get enough sleep."

"Yeah, don't we know it. I used to hate having to wake her up for that Thursday morning seven o'clock class when she stayed at the apartment. She would be so fussy."

"Where is the outhouse?" Nancy asked.

Ray pointed to it.

"I'm afraid to go by myself. Will you go with me, Cara?"

Beth told the girls, "If you don't want to use the outhouse, squat by the trees. That's what I do. No one will watch."

"I will use the outhouse," Nancy said.

Caralyn decided to use the trees instead of the outhouse. She came back and Tucker grinned.

"Why are you looking at me like that, Tuck? I bet you used the trees to take a leak. I can too."

He grinned. "You are still part tomboy, Carrie."

"Which part?" Beth asked. "She looks like all girl to me. Cara, maybe you should put on some more clothes."

Caralyn looked at herself and turned red. She glanced at Ray to see if he was looking at her, but he was busy with breakfast. She scurried back to the tent and put on a clean t-shirt along with her bra.

"I'm hungry. Is breakfast ready yet, Ray?"

"Coming right up, Caralyn."

After breakfast they set out for a bike ride. Beth took the van and acted as a support vehicle in case anyone got tired of riding. Ray, an experienced rider, knew the area well. Caralyn, Nancy and the boys followed him, but were hard pressed to keep up. Especially on the hills.

"Thanks for taking it easy on us, Ray," Tucker said. "That hill is steeper than it looks."

"Did you enjoy the ride?" Ray asked Caralyn.

"I did, but I'm afraid I will pay for it later." She rubbed her thighs. "My butt and legs will be sore tomorrow."

After lunch Ray told them about the small lake where he and Beth swam. "It's a three minute walk. Cottonwood and other trees surround most of the lake, but there is a meadow on the western edge. It's a perfect spot to spread out a blanket and work on your tan."

"Do you want to go swimming, Nancy?" Caralyn asked.

"What are the guys going to do?"

"I don't know." She yelled at Tucker, "What are you guys doing?"

"Derren and I are going for a run. Why?"

"No reason," she answered. "How about it, Nancy?"

"I'd rather work on my tan, but Ray is around."

Caralyn laughed. "You do know what he does for a living, right?"

"No, what does he do?"

"He's a photographer, and he does nude models."

Nancy wrapped her arms over her chest.

"Not always, but sometimes. Beth has modeled for him and the guys know it. He won't pay any attention to us."

Ray swam for a while before returning to camp. The girls put on their bikinis and joined Beth. After a while Beth removed her top and lay on her stomach. Tucker and Derren returned from their run and wandered to the lake.

"Did you go swimming, Cara?" Derren asked.

"There's no one around," Tucker said. "You could go skinny dipping."

Beth put on her t-shirt and sat up. "Caralyn! Did you go skinny dipping again."

"No, I took off my top last year on vacation, but I'm not doing it here."

Nancy whispered, "I would never do that."

Derren and Tucker walked to the edge of the lake.

"Do you think there's any fish in there?"

"Probably, but we don't have anything to use, and I think you need a license anyway."

"That is so nuts. I will never pay to fish."

They walked back to where the ladies were working on their tans.

"We're going back to the campsite. Are you coming with us, Cara?" Tucker asked.

"I'm going to work on my tan like Beth. I will be back later. Are you going to come back and check on me? Maybe look at me like a voyeur or peeping tom?"

"If we come back, and find you naked, we will toss you in the lake and steal your clothes."

"Not going to happen, Tucker McKay," Caralyn said.

Derren and Tucker walked back while Caralyn and Nancy worked on their tans with Beth.

"Cara, do you want me to undo your top? You could at least get a good tan on your back and get rid of your tan line."

"Okay, Beth. As long as Ray, or the boys aren't around."

"Would you be embarrassed if Ray saw you naked?" Beth asked undoing Caralyn's top.

"Yes."

"What about Tucker or Derren?"

"Probably, even though they caught me skinny dipping in Grandpa's pond when I was a kid," Caralyn answered. *I certainly wouldn't care if Tuck saw me naked again, but I don't want Derren to see me.*

"I'm not taking off my top," Nancy said. "I feel uneasy letting them see my bikini."

"Beth, can I tell you something?" Caralyn asked. "We were never close when I was a kid."

"I know, Cara, but we are closer now. You can tell me anything."

Caralyn was close to confessing she was not a virgin but decided against it. "I just want to tell you I wish I was more like you when it comes to boys."

"Cara, you don't need to be embarrassed about boys or sex. I'm sure there are lots of boys at school after you. You are so pretty. Have you dated many boys?"

"No, I've never really had a real boyfriend yet. I hang out with Tuck and Derren and their roommate, Richard, all the time. I don't want to get involved with another boy yet."

"You are still too young to get serious," Beth said. She made the natural assumption her little sister was still an innocent virgin.

They ate supper late and afterward sat around the fire roasting marshmallows.

"Do you know any ghost stories to tell us, Ray. Caralyn loves to hear ghost stories. Right, Carrie?"

175

"Tucker, you know I don't like to hear scary stories right before bedtime."

"I know, I was only teasing you."

Caralyn surprised Ray by acting so childlike. At that age Beth was already living on her own, going to college with a part-time job and making a life for herself.

"I'm going to turn in. Are you ready, Beth?" Ray asked.

"Yeah, I'm ready. Did you call home, Caralyn?"

"I did before we ate, and Nancy called her mom. Mom said I don't need to call every night unless I want to."

"Good night, everyone. See you all when the sun comes up." Beth followed Ray to their tent.

Everyone else decided to go for a walk.

"I don't want to be around if they go at it again," Tucker said as he heard laughter from the tent.

They were gone for an hour. When they returned, the camp was quiet except for the deafening sound of nature.

"I thought it was supposed to be quiet in nature. Listen to the racket," Nancy said as she listened to the crickets, frogs and other humming creatures. Even the occasional hoot of an owl.

"I'm going to bed. Are you and Caralyn going to stay up?" Tucker asked.

"I'm going to bed," Nancy said. "Are you coming, Cara?"

"Not yet. I want to stay up for a while, but not too long. Especially if we have to get up at sunrise. I thought we were on vacation. Why do we need to get up so early?"

"You can sleep late when you get home, Carrie."

Caralyn and Derren talked while watching the dying embers of the campfire. Derren added a log after Caralyn claimed she was cold. The new log caused a shower of sparks to light up the night. Soon the fire crackled with a warm orange-red glow.

"Put your arm around me, Derry, and keep me warm."

"Sit in front of me, Cara, and I'll put my arms around you. Are you still chilly even with your sweatshirt on?"

"A little bit, but I'm warming up now." She moved back into Derren, and he held her close.

176

"Do you miss Natalie?"

"A little, but I knew she wouldn't come camping even if we didn't have that big fight. She is too much of a girl to enjoy this."

"So because I can enjoy camping with a bunch of smelly guys, I am not a girl."

"You can be so funny, but that's not what I meant, Cara."

She took his arms and placed them over her chest. She held her hands over his arms and cuddled against him to keep warm as they talked. Derren didn't make a big deal about it but held her tightly.

"Are you feeling warmer now, Cara?"

"I feel warmer and should go to bed, but it feels so good by the fire. Just a few minutes more, okay? We don't get to sit by a fire at home."

"Okay, Cara. Let me know when you're ready." He leaned closer and could smell the slight aroma of pine in her hair.

They enjoyed the fire for a short time longer. Caralyn yawned and Derren told her, "It's time for bed, sleepyhead."

"Do you think it's silly I won't go swimming in front of you guys? You have seen me naked before."

"It's not silly at all, Cara. When we saw you, we were on the other side of the pond. We saw you, but not up close, you know. Just because we saw you that time doesn't mean you need to get naked in front of us all the time."

"Thanks, Derry. You are so sweet. See you in the morning."

Caralyn unzipped the tent and slipped inside. She could tell Nancy was already asleep. She undressed and slipped into her sleeping bag.

Chapter Thirty

"Cara, are you awake? I need to pee, and I don't want to go alone," Nancy said, "and I hear the boys outside."

"Give me a second, and I'll go with you," Caralyn answered.

They slipped out of their sleeping bags and put on shorts.

"I miss my bed," Nancy said. "The sleeping bags are all right, but the ground is as hard as cement."

"We could always sleep on top of the bags. It would provide a little padding," Caralyn said. "Let's go before the boys hear us."

They unzipped the tent and scooted out.

"Look who's up, Tuck," Derren said pointing at the girls.

Tucker stopped cleaning his bike, turned to look at the girls, chuckled and asked, "Where are you going, Cara?"

She made a face and said, "We have to pee."

"Watch out for snakes," Tucker hollered. "Ray caught one earlier."

Nancy froze in place. "Are there really snakes?"

"Sure! We're in the woods," Derren answered.

"I'm afraid of snakes," Nancy said reaching for Caralyn.

Tucker grinned and said, "You don't have to worry."

"Why? Were you kidding about the snakes?"

"The snakes will hide. They don't want to get peed on."

"You are so bad, Tuck. Stop teasing her," Caralyn said. "Derry will go with us. Won't you, Derry?"

"Might as well, I've got to pee, too."

"All right, I will go," Tucker added. "We might as well all water a tree at the same time."

Caralyn groaned and said, "You guys are disgusting. I'm going to go by myself so I don't have to watch you guys pissing on some poor tree."

Derren and Tucker laughed because they knew she was not afraid. She had been playing in the woods all her life.

"There's this really good bar in town with good food, live music and everyone hangs out there. Does that sound all right?" Beth asked.

"As long as I don't have to ride my bike to get there," Caralyn said. "My butt's sore from riding."

"Why?" Tucker asked. "You and Nancy spent all afternoon by the lake."

"We needed to work on our tans." Caralyn frowned at Tucker then turned to ask Beth, "Will the bar let us in?"

"Yeah, it's a family restaurant. The actual bar is at one end."

"Sounds good to me," Ray said. "I don't feel like grilling tonight."

Ray and Beth ordered a pitcher of beer and the kids shared a pitcher of Coke. They ordered two large pizzas since Derren and Tucker would devour one on their own. Later, they watched a band carry guitars, amplifiers and a drum-kit into the bar.

"Hey! I know those guys," Ray said. "They're a great cover band. They'll play three sets of danceable music. We should stay to listen."

"I'll stay if someone will dance with me," Caralyn said then turned to Derren. "Will you dance with me so Tuck can dance with Nancy?"

Nancy nudged Caralyn and whispered, "Will you stop trying to set me up with Tuck. I'm still seeing Terry Mullen, and Tucker told me he was dating Laurie something or other."

"Yeah, but you guys like each other. You should dump Terry and hook up with Tuck."

"I am not hooking up with anyone, Caralyn!"

"I didn't mean it like that. You should dance with him, and I'll make Derry stay with me."

"He's your cousin," Nancy said.

"I'm not going to sleep with him. I just want to dance and have fun that doesn't include sitting on a bicycle."

"I understand. My bottom is sore, too."

179

They listened to one set and decided to stay for the next one. Ray and Beth kept drinking and refused to dance. Caralyn danced with Derren and convinced Tucker to dance with Nancy. Caralyn noticed a guy watching her later. *Hmmmm. You look older than Derren and Tucker, but not as old as Ray.* He smiled at her, and Caralyn smiled back. After one dance Derren needed to use the bathroom. The guy approached Caralyn while she swayed to the music by herself.

"Hi, my name is Jeremiah Wilton, and I've been watching you. Would you allow me one dance?"

Caralyn looked at Derren as he walked away. She turned to Jeremiah and said, "My name is Caralyn, and I would love to dance."

They danced for a few minutes, and then the band took a break.

"Did I hear you mention Stockton Woods earlier?" Jeremiah asked.

"Yes, that's where I live. Have you heard of it?"

"My grandmother lived there until she passed away."

"Get out! Seriously!" Caralyn shrieked. "What was her name? I've lived there all my life."

"All twenty years of it?" he asked.

She grinned and answered, "Sneaky, huh? You want to know how old I am."

"I do, and I will start by admitting I am twenty-five." He waited but Caralyn didn't tell him her age. "My grandmother's name was Genevieve Brown."

"No way!" Caralyn poked his arm.

"It was," he answered rubbing his arm.

"My grandma was Florence Jackson. She and Mrs. Brown were good friends. Have you ever been to Stockton Woods?"

"Not for at least ten years. Maybe longer. I think I might have been to your grandmother's house." He described a visit and what he remembered about the house.

"Amazing! That's Grandma's house."

Jeremiah said, "It proves how small the world is now."

Caralyn told him about their camping trip and other things. Jeremiah listened with interest and asked, "Would you be able to meet me here Friday night?"

"I think I could." She noticed Derren and Tucker watching her. "I should really get back to my friends."

"I will be here Friday, and I'd love to dance with you again."

"I'll do my best to be here."

Jeremiah shook her hand as she left.

"Who was that guy, Cara? Do you know him?" Nancy asked.

"His name is Jeremiah Wilton, and I just met him. He's nice, and I agreed to meet him here Friday night."

"You made a date with a total stranger!"

"It's not a real date, and he's not a stranger anymore. You'll never guess, but his grandmother knew Grandma Florence. Isn't that a weird coincidence?"

"Yeah, too weird." Nancy stared at Jeremiah. "How do you know he's telling the truth?"

"He told me about visiting Grandma's house when he was a kid. He described the house in detail. How would he be able to do that if he hadn't been there?"

Nancy thought about it for a moment. "Okay, so maybe his grandma and Grandma Florence knew each other, doesn't mean he is okay."

"Am I detecting a bit of jealousy because a handsome older man finds me attractive?" Caralyn asked then grinned.

"I'm not jealous, Cara. He looks devious to me. He reminds me of my cousin."

Caralyn glanced at Jeremiah. "He does look like an older version of Bryce."

"Are you going to tell Tucker? He won't like you seeing an older man."

Caralyn looked at Tucker and Derren as they were sitting with their backs to her. "I will need an excuse for someone to bring me here Friday."

"I'm coming with you," Nancy insisted. "Either that or you aren't coming."

"That's okay. I won't mind if you're with me."

On the way back to the campground, Caralyn mentioned she wanted to come back Friday.

"Why? Did that old guy ask you for a date?" Tucker teased never suspecting the truth.

"He did for your information," Caralyn said.

"What? No way, Caralyn," Tucker said.

"Do I need to ask your permission before I make a date?"

"Yes, you do," Tucker replied.

"Fine! I don't care. Will you and Derren come with me and Nancy Friday night in case I want to leave early?"

"You mean in case Jerry turns out to be a jerk?"

"His name is Jeremiah and not because I think he might be a jerk, but just in case I don't want to stay as late as he does."

"In case he's a jerk," Tucker teased.

"All right. In case he's a jerk; which I'm sure he's not."

Caralyn wore her bikini as she got ready for her date.

"Since you're taking another cold shower, I guess I won't have to worry about you being horny," Tucker teased.

"That only works on guys. Girls don't get horny."

Tucker laughed and said, "Yeah, right."

"Will you turn around while I wash my private areas. I don't want anyone to catch you looking at me."

Tucker turned around so she could finish her shower.

"Thank you, Tuck. I'm done."

"Here's your towel, Carrie. Can I go now? I need to help Ray with dinner."

"Thank you for being so good to me, Tuck."

"You're welcome." Tucker left to help Ray.

Caralyn shivered as she raced back to the tent. A few minutes later she stumbled out of the tent as she tripped on the mesh opening.

Derren and Tucker were watching and laughed. "Carrie, you look about as graceful as an elephant on roller skates."

"Oh, knock it off. I forgot the entrance sticks up like that, and I think I scraped my knee.."

"Wow! Look at you." Ray whistled.

"I didn't know you packed a dress, Cara," Tucker said.

"How does it look?" She spun around to give them a good look.

"You look amazing," Ray said.

"It is kinda short though." Tucker checked to see how far above her knee it came.

"She looks great, Tucker, and why shouldn't she show off her legs? She has great looking legs—so tan and slim," Ray said as he gave her a thumbs up.

"Thank you for sticking up for me, Ray."

"You're welcome, Caralyn, and remember if that guy lays a hand on you, I will shoot him."

"Yes, Daddy, I will remember."

Tucker, Derren and Nancy drove Caralyn back into town.

She instructed them, "Now don't let on you know me and don't keep staring at us, okay?"

"Yes, your highness. We will obey your every command," Tucker teased.

"Tuck, you can be such a dork sometimes."

"You do remember he saw you with us before, don't you?" Tucker asked.

"He might not recognize or remember you. He only saw you for a few seconds, and I don't think he saw Derren at all. Jeremiah will bring me back to the campground. You don't have to wait up, but you probably will."

"You know I will, Carrie. Have a good time, but not too good a time. Know what I mean?"

"I'm not going to do anything with him, Tuck. Don't worry about me." Caralyn hustled inside to find Jeremiah while Tucker, Derren and Nancy waited outside for the five minutes she demanded. She found him alone at a table.

"Caralyn, I'm glad you made it. I was afraid you would forget about me."

"I didn't forget about you, but I'm sorry I am running a bit late. I got a ride from my cousin, and he missed a turn and we got a little lost."

"You look captivating tonight."

"Thank you, Jeremiah. That's sweet of you to say." Caralyn remembered the cold shower she endured to get ready as she waited in vain for him to pull out her chair.

"I love your dress. The color brings out your eyes."

She shrugged and sat down. "It's just an old dress."

"Too many young ladies your age dress in jeans and t-shirts all the time. I appreciate a young lady who knows how to dress appropriately."

She smiled at him. *I'm glad I decided to pack this dress. I didn't think I would have a chance to wear it.*

Jeremiah took out his pocket organizer. "Do you have a phone number I can use to stay in touch. I have an email address, do you?"

"I do. I'll write it down for you."

They ordered food and Jeremiah ordered a pitcher of beer. "I know you are not old enough to drink, but you can try it if you want."

She remembered the promise she made to Mom and Dad not to drink. She put a hand over her empty glass. "Thanks, but I will stick to pop if you don't mind."

Jeremiah and Caralyn spent the next hour learning more about each other. Caralyn kept looking at Tucker and Derren and frowning at them. They tried to hide the fact they were watching her by turning away every time she glanced in their direction.

"Jeremiah, excuse me. I need to use the restroom."

"I'll be here when you return."

She stopped at Tucker's table, made sure Jeremiah wasn't looking and slipped in next to Derren.

"You aren't drinking beer, are you?" Nancy asked. "You are underage."

Caralyn shook her head. "Pop. What are you guys doing? Can't you see I'm enjoying myself?"

"We aren't doing anything, Cara. We are only keeping an eye on you in case you need our help to get away from that guy," Tucker answered.

"I'm fine, and I don't need to be rescued by you yahoos."

"Hear that, Derren? We are yahoos now."

"Is a yahoo better than a bozo?" Derren asked trying to keep a straight face.

"No, I think a bozo is better, but a doofus is better yet."

Nancy rolled her eyes.

"Come on, Tuck. Please don't treat me like a baby. I am having fun. Nothing is going to happen."

"All right, Carrie. We will stay here until eleven then head back to the campground. You have until then to decide if you need a ride."

"Thank you, Tuck."

Caralyn watched Tucker leave shortly after eleven. She turned to Jeremiah and said, " I hate to remind you, but I promised my sister I would return before midnight."

"We can leave now if you're ready. I know it's not midnight yet, but maybe we could..."

"I don't mind if we get back early." She smiled at him and thought he might kiss her when they were alone in his car.

Jeremiah brought her back to the campground. They stopped and parked out of sight, but she suspected everyone heard Jeremiah's car struggling up the hill.

Jeremiah turned off the engine. "I had a really good time with you, Caralyn. I know there's a difference in our ages now, but in a few years it will not matter. I want to stay in touch and see where our relationship leads."

"I loved being with you, Jeremiah, and I want to keep in touch, too. I don't think the difference in our ages is a big deal. I'm used to being around older people."

Jeremiah leaned close and kissed her.

"I didn't expect that, but I liked it," she said.

"I don't hesitate when I want something."

After a few more kisses, Jeremiah dropped her at the campsite.

"I expect you to keep in touch, Caralyn. I really think we could have a future together."

"I will, I promise. I really enjoyed being with you because you are so much more mature than my other friends. I think you will be a good influence for me."

She kissed him goodbye and got out of the car. She watched as he drove away.

"How did it go, Carrie?" Tucker surprised her as he quietly stole up behind her.

"Tuck, don't do that. You scared the crap out of me."

"Sorry, Carrie."

"I had a pleasant evening, Tuck. He was a gentleman the whole night."

"Yeah, we watched to make sure."

They walked to the campsite and sat by the fire ring. Tucker jabbed at a log and the fire returned to life.

"I know you heard his car when he brought me back. We stopped for a little bit, and, yes, he kissed me, but he didn't try anything more."

"I'm glad you had a good time, Carrie. Is he a good kisser?"

She smacked his arm. "We didn't kiss too much, so I don't know how good a kisser he is. Maybe you should kiss me so I can compare while his kisses are fresh in my mind, or have you been kissing Nancy?"

"We talked but nothing else. She likes Terry now."

"She likes you more, you dweeb."

"Maybe."

Beth opened up her tent and stepped out. She could see the silhouettes of Caralyn and Tucker by the fire and walked toward them. They didn't hear her at first, but finally Caralyn saw her.

"We weren't doing anything, Beth. Really!"

"It's all right, Cara. How was your date?" Beth moved to stand next to Caralyn.

"Productive. I learned a lot about Jeremiah. He talked about his goal of becoming an investment banker. He explained about organizing one's time to be the most productive, and he gave me several examples of how I could appear more mature. Older men don't treat me like a baby like Tucker and Derren."

Tucker stared at her. *That sounds like the weirdest date in history.*

"Ray really likes you, Cara. He thinks of you as a perfect little sister."

Tucker snorted and Caralyn elbowed him.

"You love him a lot, don't you, Beth?"

"Yeah, I do."

"Do you think you will ever get married?"

"We talk about it. I think we will get married when we are ready for kids." Beth smiled at them. "I'm going to take a walk until I get sleepy again. See you two in the morning."

"Night, Beth," Tucker said.

"Do you think she knows?" Caralyn asked. "That we had sex, I mean."

He shrugged. "No clue, but she might suspect something."

They stayed by the fire for a few more minutes before getting into their tents.

"What's this guy really like?" Nancy asked while Caralyn undressed.

"Jeremiah is mature. He doesn't treat me like a child, and he respects my goal of becoming a writer."

"I know I don't know him, but I get a weird vibe from him."

"He's not like Bryce."

"I hope not," Nancy said. "Bryce got a girl pregnant last year and paid for her abortion."

"You're kidding!" Caralyn shuddered. "I don't want to think about that. It will never happen to me."

After her vacation, Caralyn and Jeremiah talked and sent lengthy emails back and forth. Despite the fact he lived six hours away, his influence, including suggestions about organizing her time, affected her, and she became infatuated because of his maturity. They promised to see each other before school started.

"Did you tell your parents about Jeremiah?" Nancy asked on the way to visit Nancy's aunt in McHenry Hills.

"No, and now I feel guilty."

"You should tell them," Nancy suggested.

Nancy's aunt lived close to Six Flags Great America, so Caralyn arranged to meet Jeremiah there. Jeremiah brought Grant along to keep Nancy occupied, but the plan backfired because Nancy developed an immediate dislike for Jeremiah's friend.

"I want to go on the rides with you, Cara."

"Why? Don't you like Grant?"

"Not in the least! He made a remark about us being 'Daisy Maes from Hicksville,' and I don't trust him."

"We can ride the roller coasters together because Jeremiah doesn't like to ride them. I want to ride every one."

"You sound more excited about visiting the park than the opportunity to spend time with Jeremiah," Nancy said.

Caralyn shrugged. "He's just a guy. I love the coasters."

Disappointment flooded Jeremiah's thoughts because he wouldn't have time to know Caralyn more intimately. He observed her acting like a tomboy and that disturbed him. He made a mental note to talk with her about childish behavior.

Nancy told Caralyn, "I don't really trust Jeremiah, but he really likes you, Cara. Do you think of him as a potential boyfriend?"

"I think so. I know he's interested in me that way, but he hasn't tried to do anything other than kiss me. What I really like is the fact he treats me like an adult and not like a kid the way Tuck and Derren do. They drive me crazy at times with their silly teasing. They need to grow up."

"How old is he?"

"He's twenty-five, and he's so mature and sophisticated. Isn't it wonderful?"

"If you say so."

Tucker expressed a bit of jealousy over her relationship with Jeremiah. Caralyn confronted him one day after he overheard her talking to him on the phone.

"I would appreciate some privacy when I am talking to Jeremiah."

Tucker snidely commented, "What do you see in that old man? He acts like he's fifty."

"Tucker, why are you acting like this? I like Jeremiah, and he likes me. He treats me with respect and not as a child like you."

He put his hands on her shoulders and looked into her eyes. "Cara, you may be the most intelligent person I know, but sometimes you don't have the common sense of a moron."

She smacked his stomach. "Screw you, Tucker."

"I don't trust him, Cara, and I think he wants to get you into bed."

"Well, you couldn't be more wrong, and you don't any room to talk. Not once did he behave like anything other than a true gentleman." She walked away in a huff.

Tucker tried to think of a way to find out more about Jeremiah. Caralyn and Tucker's relationship became strained, and she convinced herself that any romantic interest she once felt for Tucker had waned. She spent the rest of the summer working at The Curve, and Tucker headed to another basketball camp. When school started, Caralyn didn't spend much time at the apartment with Tucker, Derren and Richard. She concentrated on her classes and her new boyfriend, Jeremiah Wilton.

Chapter Thirty-One

"He's not that old, Tuck! In a few years it won't matter if he is a few years older than me anyway," Caralyn told Tucker as they walked to her dorm after dinner.

"In a few years! Are you planning on getting married to him already?" Tucker angrily asked as he slammed his hand against the elevator up button.

"No! Not yet, but maybe in a few years, we might." She avoided looking at him.

They didn't speak as they waited for the elevator. The doors slid open and they entered. She waited for him to push the button for the fifth floor, but he didn't.

"I'll get it myself." She pushed the button and turned her back to him.

They left the elevator, and he followed her down the hall. "I can't believe it. You hardly know him, and you are planning to spend your life with him."

"We will have time to get to know each other." She looked for her key in her backpack. "You should go now because I need to call Jeremiah. We talk to each other at seven o'clock on Tuesdays."

"What time do you talk to him on Thursdays?" Tucker asked facetiously.

"Let me check my organizer. Seven-thirty on Thursday. He has a later class and..."

"I was kidding, Cara. You have lost your sense of humor since you met this guy, and what's with this organizer thing? Is every moment of your week planned to the last second? How can you be like that?"

"Jeremiah has an organizer, and he helped me set up mine. No, not every second is planned. I plan things in fifteen minute segments. It helps me keep on track and manage my time more efficiently. Time matters, Tucker."

Tucker looked at Caralyn with a puzzled expression. "I don't even know you anymore, Carrie. You have changed so much since last year."

190

"I'm becoming more mature and responsible. I am becoming an adult, Tucker McKay. You should try it."

"Caralyn, you are seventeen! You're still a young girl."

"I am not! I am a young lady, so there." Caralyn stuck her tongue out at Tucker, marched into her room and slammed the door in his face.

With his nose only an inch from the door Tucker muttered, "Where have you gone, Carrie, and who is inhabiting your body now?"

Richard asked Tucker one night, "What has Caralyn been doing lately? She hasn't come over to see us all week and avoids us at dinnertime."

"Yeah! What's up with her? I saw her coming out of the journalism building a couple of days ago wearing glasses and she had her hair done up like an old lady. She was wearing a pant suit or some old-fashioned thing," Derren replied.

Tucker shook his head. "It's Jeremiah. He told her she needed to change her appearance to look older and more mature so her professors will take her seriously. She's not the same Caralyn anymore."

"That really sucks!" Richard answered as he grabbed a beer from the fridge.

"Yeah! Tell me about it," Tucker answered. "I didn't like Jeremiah from the beginning, and now she acts like she's under his control or something. I think he brainwashed her."

After dinner Friday evening, Tucker knocked on Caralyn's dorm room door. He had hardly seen her in the last month and neither had Derren nor Richard.

She put her hand over the phone and hollered, "Just a second, I'm on the phone." She stood up. "Hang on, Jeremiah. I need to open the door." She let Tucker in and whispered, "I'll be ready in a minute. Have a seat, be patient and don't try to eavesdrop." She continued her conversation with Jeremiah but spoke softly so Tucker couldn't hear.

191

Tucker sat on her bed and picked up the stuffed bear from next to her pillow. He knew she had cherished this bear since she was a little girl. Caralyn turned around to see what Tucker was doing.

"Put him down, Tuck! And get off of my bed. You'll wrinkle the covers."

Tucker stared at Caralyn. *What has gotten into you?*

"No, not you, Jeremiah. My ride home just got here, and I was talking to him." Caralyn turned away so Tucker couldn't hear her as she finished her conversation with Jeremiah. "I miss you, too. I will talk to you Monday at our normal time." She listened to Jeremiah for a moment and then answered, "I love you more." She giggled then whispered, "No! I love you more."

Tucker could barely hear Caralyn's part of the conversation and imagined what Jeremiah was saying. Caralyn hung up and turned to face Tucker.

"Will you put Teddy back where he belongs and get off my bed, please. I don't mess up your bed, do I?"

"You can if you want, Carrie. You can mess up my bed anytime. I don't mind."

"I'm not going to mess up your bed, Tucker. Please! Can we just go? I have work to do when we get home. I have two papers to start and important reading to finish. Let me check my organizer." She opened it and read aloud. "Friday night, two hours of studying, followed by a half hour with Mom and Dad. Saturday morning, get up at 6:30. Dress and be ready by 6:45." She glanced at Tucker, who stared at her with a blank expression. "What?"

"Nothing, I was wondering how much time you allow for, say, going to the bathroom and stuff like that. Do you have a set time to take care of nature calls?"

Caralyn gave Tucker a look of disgust. "Don't be ridiculous! How can I plan that?" She checked her organizer again before tossing it into her backpack. "Well, what are you waiting for, Tucker? We are already twenty-two minutes late getting started." She checked the time. "Will you carry my laundry basket, please?"

"Sure," Tucker picked up the basket of dirty clothes and saw her underwear on top. He picked up a pair of panties and twirled it around on his finger.

Caralyn turned to see what he was doing. "Will you put them back and stop acting so immature. I'm sure you have seen girls underwear before."

"I think I have seen you in this specific pair before, Carrie."

She grabbed her underwear and stuffed them back in the basket. "Tucker, leave my panties alone. Let's get going, and when are you going to stop calling me that childish name. We are not children anymore. My name is Caralyn Ann Dawson, and I would appreciate it if you use my proper name."

"Yes, of course, Ms. Dawson. Anything you wish." Tucker was totally convinced Caralyn had been brainwashed by Jeremiah somehow and hoped she would return to normal soon. He missed her so much.

On the trip home Caralyn read her textbook and ignored Tucker's attempts to draw her into conversation.

"Did you hear me?" Tucker asked.

"What did you say? Can't you see I'm busy?"

"I asked why you decided to wear a dress for the ride home? Especially one that looks like Mom should be wearing it." He asked while passing a slow moving flat-bed semi.

"I want to look grown up and responsible. Like a mature adult, and Daddy likes it when I dress nicely," she answered without looking up from her book. "You should try it sometime."

"None of your dresses fit me."

She rolled her eyes but didn't respond.

Tucker decided to let her read. A few minutes later Caralyn scratched her leg. She glanced at Tucker and noticed him looking.

"You've seen my leg before. Why are you staring at it now?"

"Because I can."

She laughed for the first time during the ride. "I had an itch, and I needed to scratch it. I wasn't showing my leg to excite you."

193

"Oh, I'm not excited. If you lifted your dress higher and let me see, I might get excited."

"Don't be so gross. You need to keep your eyes on the road, and don't be thinking about my underwear, all right?"

"Fine, I won't think about your white panties with pink polka dots."

"I'm not wearing that pair."

"Yes, you are."

"No, I am not! Please just drive."

"Pink polka dots, I know it," Tucker teased her for a while.

"Fine! Here look!" She lifted her dress along the side. "See! They are white with purple stripes. Are you satisfied now?"

"My mistake, Ms. Dawson. I thought for sure today was the day you were supposed to wear the pink polka dot ones. What does it say in your organizer?"

"I don't put that in my organizer." They looked at each other, and she smiled at him. "Did that excite you?"

"No, not really. I am too mature to get aroused by seeing your underwear, baby girl."

"I am not a baby! You might think you're my big brother, but I am not a baby anymore, and I'm especially not your sister. Concentrate on your driving and let me read."

"I will if you fix your dress so your leg isn't showing."

She fixed her dress and resumed reading. She had trouble concentrating as she thought about the first night they made love. She looked at him, but he was watching the road. She wondered if he ever thought about that night the way she did.

"Tuck," she whispered.

"What, Cara? I mean, Ms. Dawson."

"Nothing. I was thinking about something."

"Are you all right?"

"I'm okay, and I'm sorry I got mad at you for calling me Carrie. You can still call me Carrie. I don't mind, really."

Tucker looked at her and smiled. *Maybe the real Caralyn still exists after all.*

Chapter Thirty-Two

"Hi, Mom! Hi, Daddy! We're home."

Mom took off her white apron and placed it over a kitchen chair. "Hello, Caralyn. How are classes going?"

"I will tell you all about it at dinnertime. Do you need any help in the kitchen?"

"Everything is about ready, dear. You can help your father set the table if you want."

Caralyn talked to her parents about politics, the local school system, the economy and tried to act like a mature adult.

Jim whispered to his wife, "Why is she acting as if she were thirty-years-old instead of a teenage tomboy?"

"I'm not sure. Maybe she will explain while we eat," Sarah answered.

After they finished dinner, but before they left the table, Caralyn announced, "I met someone, and we are getting married."

Mom stared at her in shock. Dad nearly choked on his sweet tea. Tucker dropped his last bite of chocolate cake on the floor.

"What did you say, honey?" Mom eventually regained the use of her voice.

"Mom, I met this guy in the summer, and we are going to get married. Not right away, but after I graduate."

Dad looked at Caralyn and Tucker as if this was a bad dream. Tucker's face drained of all color.

"Excuse me, Caralyn, but did you say you were getting married?" Dad shook his head to help clear his ears. "My ears don't seem to be working right."

"Yes, Daddy! Isn't that great news?"

Mr. McKay looked at Caralyn and saw the little girl who used to sit on his lap so he could read her a story. "Caralyn, you can't get married. I won't allow it. You aren't even old enough to be dating. I absolutely forbid it. You are grounded for a month."

"Daddy! You can't ground me. I'm in college."

"There is no way you are getting married now or in the future," Dad said. "The idea is preposterous."

Tucker listened quietly without saying a word.

"Let's discuss this sensibly like adults, Jim."

"I will not discuss it sensibly, and she is not an adult." He pointed at Caralyn. "She is barely old enough to drive. She isn't old enough to vote or even start her own checking account. No way on earth she is old enough to get married." He smacked the table. "I absolutely forbid it."

Mom stared at Dad until he calmed down.

"What is this boy's name, honey?" Mom asked calmly.

"His name is Jeremiah Wilton, and he's not a boy, he's a man."

"A man! A man! How old is this man?" Dad asked angrily as he fought to keep his emotions under control.

"He's twenty-five, Daddy, and he's finishing his master's degree in Banking. He's going to be an investment counselor with his own company."

"Young lady, I forbid you to ever see him again. He's twice your age." Dad waved his hands, sat back in his chair and then folded his arms across his chest to close the matter forever.

"Now, dear, calm down. Twenty-five is not twice her age. Tucker, have you met Jeremiah?"

"I've seen him, but I haven't been introduced to him." *What is going on? Where did this come from, Carrie?*

"What did you think of this man?" Dad asked.

"Daddy! It doesn't matter what Tucker thinks about Jeremiah. It only matters what I think, and I think he is incredibly mature and level-headed."

"Mature! Level-Headed?" Dad waved his hands again. "What does that even mean? You are not going back to that school. You are enrolling at Dickinson so I can keep an eye on you. That's it! End of discussion." Dad crossed his arms over his chest again and scowled at everyone.

"I am not changing schools, and you can not dictate how I live my life." Caralyn left the table in tears.

"Now see what you've done," Sarah glared at her husband.

"May I be excused? I need to get some fresh air," Tucker asked. "I think I've been transported to the twilight zone."

"Yes, but please don't stay out too late," Mom nodded.

Tucker left the table and headed outside.

Mom shook her head.

"What? She can't get married," Dad insisted.

"She did mention getting married after she graduates."

"I guess I didn't hear that part," Dad said.

"You do realize you overreacted, right? You treated her like a child. She's a young lady with a mind of her own. An especially good mind, I might add. You treated her like she was ten. You need to calm down and apologize to her."

"But..."

Mom waved a finger. "No, buts."

Dad sighed and looked at a family photo on the wall taken six years ago. "Fine. I will talk to her."

Mom stood up. "I think you need to apologize to her."

"But she's..."

"Go! Now! Apologize!"

"Fine! I'm going," he muttered under his breath.

Dad knocked on the door to her room and walked in. Caralyn was crying on the bed. "I'm sorry if I have been treating you like a child, Cara. I know you are growing up, and I should accept that fact. Now tell me more about your Jerry." He sat next to her.

"It's Jeremiah, Daddy. No one calls him Jerry. He hates it, and he is so smart," Caralyn told Dad all about Jeremiah. "So we aren't getting married for three years yet, and I will be through with college."

"When do we get to meet Jer... er... Jeremiah?"

"Over the holidays while we are on break. He wants to see Grandma's house again."

Dad furrowed his brow. "Again?"

"Oh, I should have mentioned..." she explained the details.

"We will look forward to meeting him, honey."

"Oh, Daddy! I love you, and I'm sorry I sprung this on you without any warning."

Before he headed to bed, Tucker knocked on the door to Caralyn's room. She sat at her desk in her pajamas working on a school project. He put his hands on her shoulders and she looked up.

"Cara, why didn't you tell me you and Jeremiah had talked about getting married?"

She swiveled to face him. "I didn't tell you because I was afraid you would tell me I was too young to think about getting married."

He chuckled and said, "You're right. That's probably what I would have said. I think you need to get to know him better before you announce to the world you are engaged."

"Tuck, we aren't officially engaged. We have been talking about it. He hasn't really asked me, but I can tell he wants to. Maybe I shouldn't have told Mom and Dad the way I did."

"No doubt."

"They must think I'm ready to elope with him as soon as I get back to school. We have made some plans, but nothing set in stone. I'm sorry if I haven't been nice to you lately. I have had so much on my mind, and I've been trying to prove to Jeremiah that I'm not a child. Maybe I've been trying to prove it to myself, too."

"Carrie, you know I love you, and I don't want to see you get hurt."

"I know you do, and I appreciate it. If it happens that Jeremiah and I get married; it won't be for at least three years. By then we will know each other much better. We haven't even been intimate with each other yet."

"That's good to know," Tucker sighed.

"Jeremiah suggested I get a more mature hairstyle. What do you think, Tuck?"

"I like your long hair." He ran his fingers through her long hair. "It's easy to pull on it."

"Don't."

"Wouldn't think of it," he said moving his hand away.

"I should tell Mom and Dad Jeremiah hasn't asked me to marry him yet, so they don't worry about me doing something foolish like eloping."

"They would appreciate that." He told her as he kissed her forehead and then tried to kiss her mouth.

She turned her head. "No, Tucker. Please don't kiss me like that."

"Sorry, Carrie. I'm sorry." He hurried out of the room, out of the house and sprinted down the street.

Caralyn waited a few minutes. *Oh, Bubby, I'm so sorry I didn't tell you before. You are going to hate me now.* She closed her book, walked out of her room and knocked on her parents bedroom door.

"Come in," Mom said.

Caralyn sat on the bed to talk to them about Jeremiah.

"...so he hasn't really proposed, but we kinda talked about a pre-pre-engagement agreement."

"That's better, dear. You need to concentrate on finishing college. Then if you and Jeremiah are still together..."

"Mom, we will be together. He assured me of that."

Caralyn and Jeremiah made plans to get together at the holiday break at the end of the semester. Jeremiah wanted Caralyn to come up and stay with him at his apartment, but she wanted him to come home with her to meet the McKays first. Jeremiah used every persuasive argument he could think of, and Caralyn finally agreed to visit him first, and then he would go home with her. She spent time with Tucker at the guys' apartment and let it slip one night she was going to spend part of the holiday break at Jeremiah's apartment in Meyersdale.

"Caralyn, you can't go up there by yourself. He will take advantage of you," Tucker said.

"You mean like you did!?"

Tucker looked at her with obvious disappointment.

"I'm sorry, Tuck. I didn't mean that. What we did was because I wanted it."

"We both wanted it."

"You didn't take advantage of me. I probably took advantage of you. But back to the other thing. I will be eighteen in a few days, and I will be able to make my own decisions. I could elope with him if I wanted."

"You aren't planning to do that are you?"

"No! I'm merely saying I could if I wanted. I'm not going to do anything crazy, Tuck."

"Are you saying spending time with Jeremiah in his apartment by yourself is not crazy?"

"He's not going to rape me, Tucker! He wouldn't do that. We are going to take things slow. We will have a few days to get to know each other more intimately."

Tucker looked at her incredulously. "You mean he will have a few days to screw you as much as he wants."

"Get out now!" she screamed. "Go home!"

He looked at the apartment. "I am home."

"Oh, right," she said with a sigh. "Tucker, I am not a virgin as you well know. If I want to sleep with my fiancee, that is my decision. I think it's a perfectly logical thing to do. I believe two people should get to know each other in as many ways as possible before they get married. After graduation I will probably move in with him. That way we will get accustomed to each other's habits."

"I don't want to argue with you, Carrie. I hope you know what you're doing."

"Thank you for your concern, Tucker, but I can take care of myself."

Tucker didn't trust Jeremiah, and knew he better think of a way to keep an eye on Caralyn.

Chapter Thirty-Three

Caralyn's eighteenth birthday fell on a Thursday. She walked out of her last class of the day and saw Derren and Tucker waiting for her.

"Hey, Cara. Happy birthday," Derren said with a smile.

She smiled back and then looked shyly at Tucker.

"Happy birthday, Caralyn," Tucker mentioned. "Are you doing anything special for dinner tonight?" *Are you going to spend the evening talking to Jeremiah?*

"I don't really have any special plans. Why?"

Tucker scrutinized the photograph of the first building on campus and didn't respond.

Derren sensed Tucker's discomfort. "Would you allow us to take you to dinner? You can choose the place."

Even though she had been trying to act more mature and dress accordingly, she was thrilled the guys were taking her out for her birthday.

"Can I really pick the place?" She twirled her hair.

"You can pick the place, Cara. Wherever you want," Derren offered.

She put a finger to her mouth and thought about it. "I want to try the Texas Roadhouse." She looked at Tucker because it was the place they ate dinner the night they first made love. "Is it too expensive?"

He smiled because he remembered how pretty she looked that night in her new dress. "Texas Roadhouse it is. Should we get reservations?"

"It shouldn't be too busy on a Thursday," Derren answered.

"We'll pick you up at 6:30, okay?" Tucker told her. "Richard wants to come. I hope that's all right."

She nodded. "What should I wear, Tucker? Are you expecting me to dress up or is it going to be real casual?"

"You can wear whatever you want, Cara. It's your birthday after all."

She showered and tried to decide what to wear. First she put on an old pair of jeans because she figured the guys would not get dressed up at all. *But what if they dress up? I'll look out of place.* She checked the closet and pulled out something new. She put on a nicer pair of slacks and a top with a jacket Jeremiah had suggested she buy so she could look more mature. She looked at herself in the mirror. *I look silly! I don't think Mom would even wear this outfit. It looks old-fashioned. I never should have bought it. Such a waste of money.* She removed it and looked in the closet again. In the corner she saw 'the dress.' *Maybe Tucker won't remember this is the same dress,* she thought as she grabbed it.

At 6:30 the doorbell rang. "Come on in! The door's unlocked."

The door opened and all three guys walked in. She finished in the bathroom and walked out to let the guys see her. She looked at Tucker and knew immediately he remembered the dress.

Derren and Richard whistled. Tucker looked for her teddy bear.

"Caralyn, you look fantastic! Is that a new dress? I've never seen it before," Richard said.

"I'm ready." She spotted her organizer and was about to pick it up when she looked at Tucker. He saw the organizer and sighed. She decided to leave it at home. "I'm not bringing my purse since I assume you guys are buying."

"We are indeed, Ms. Dawson. We pooled our resources and came up with twenty-five dollars for the night."

Caralyn replied in a higher pitched voice than normal. "Twenty-five dollars won't buy us more than a house salad! We should choose somewhere cheaper."

"Maybe we can come up with a little more, Cara," Derren smiled at her. They headed downstairs and bumped into Trent Cussler in the lobby.

"Caralyn, you look different tonight. What is it? Oh yeah! You fixed your hair differently," he teased and then smiled at her. "Happy birthday, Cara."

"Thank you, Trent. I'm surprised you remembered."

202

On the way to the restaurant she sat in the back with Derren as Tucker drove and Richard sat up front with him. When they were seated, Caralyn sat beside Derren in the booth. Richard sat directly across from her with Tucker next to him. She kept glancing at Tucker to see if he was upset with her or something, but she couldn't tell. They placed their orders and Richard offered a toast.

"To the most beautiful girl to ever come out of Stockton Woods."

He meant it as a compliment, but Caralyn teased him. "There haven't been that many girls to come out of Stockton Woods."

"All right. How about this. To the prettiest girl to ever come to New Lebanon."

Caralyn smiled, "That is much better, Richard. Thank you." She sat close to Derren as they talked.

Richard regaled them with stories about his week. Tucker kept quiet. He kept looking at Caralyn, and she smiled shyly at him.

She smoothed out her dress and glanced at Tucker. *He must be upset with me because I'm wearing this dress.*

I wish she would be like this all the time. Tucker sipped his Coke. *This is the Caralyn I love.*

"I told the professor I didn't agree because the economy will always suffer fluctuations," Richard said.

I can't remember what time I'm scheduled to call Jeremiah. I wish I had my organizer with me. Caralyn fretted.

Tucker picked up one of the rolls from the wicker basket. *What will I do if she doesn't like the present I bought her.*

Richard continued, "I doubt if the professor even knows my name, so I'm not too worried."

Their entrees arrived, and they stopped talking.

"Make sure you save room for dessert, Cara," Derren reminded her.

She leaned against him. "Should I take the rest of my filet home?"

"You might want to, or you could let me take it home," Derren said as he grinned.

"You ate all of your steak, and now you want mine. What a pig."

"I'm ready for dessert," Derren said. Anyone else ready?"

Tucker caught their waiter's attention, and he brought them a small cake with the candles already lit.

"Make a wish, Caralyn," Richard said.

She closed her eyes, made a wish and blew out the candles. She looked at Tucker and smiled.

Derren cut the cake and gave her the first piece. As she was ready to take a bite, Derren used his finger to put frosting on her nose. "I remember a birthday a long time ago. You ended up with birthday cake all over your face. Do you remember that, Carrie?"

"I remember it, Derry. You were the one who got the cake all over my face. Maybe I should return the favor." She swiped her finger through the frosting, grinned and wiped it on his mouth.

"Ummm! It tastes good. Thanks, pipsqueak."

She kissed Derren on the cheek and whispered in his ear, "Thank you so much. I love you a lot, Derry, and I didn't mind you calling me Carrie tonight. Just don't make it a habit."

"Wouldn't think of it."

Tucker offered to take her upstairs when they got back to her dorm. "I'll be right back, guys."

Derren and Richard got out of the car. "Take your time. Richard and I are going to walk home. He needs the exercise."

"Good night, Cara. I hope you had a good birthday." Richard stared at her until Derren nudged him in the side.

Tucker and Caralyn rode the elevator in silence and avoided eye contact. Tucker walked her to her room and stood behind her as she unlocked the door.

"Can I come in for a second, Cara?"

"Of course you can." *I'm not going to call Jeremiah now. I haven't been thinking about him the entire night.* "Thank you for dinner. It was thoughtful of you guys."

"You're welcome. You look so pretty tonight. Like you did the first time you wore that dress."

"I hope you don't mind that I wore it again. I didn't know if you would remember, and if you did, afraid you would be upset."

"I'll never forget that dress. You let Derren call you Carrie tonight. Were you aware of that?"

"Yes, and I hope you didn't mind, Bubby."

"I didn't." He reached in his pocket and pulled out a small gift wrapped box. "I got you something, Cara. It's not much. I hope you like it." He handed it to her.

She smiled at him and carefully opened the gift. Inside was a small charm for her bracelet—a small teddy bear.

"Oh, Tuck! This is perfect. I love it!"

"I found it a month ago."

"Could you put it on my bracelet, please?"

He attached the charm to her bracelet. She hugged him and began to sob.

"It's all right, Carrie. I can take it back if you don't like it." Tucker began to cry softly also.

"You better not," she whispered.

They held each other tightly without it becoming sexual. She thought about how much he had meant to her over the years as she looked at the teddy bear nestled against the pillows on her bed. She remembered when they would play with it even though Tucker would rather be outside playing ball.

He looked at the teddy bear on her bed and remembered how they used to pretend the bear was their baby. Without saying a single word they both remembered the same moment in time.

Finally, Caralyn spoke up, "You were so quiet tonight, Tuck. I was afraid you were mad at me."

"I wasn't mad at you, Carrie. I didn't know if you would like my present."

"You always get me the perfect gift, Tuck. How could I not love it?" She looked into his eyes and smiled.

He leaned down and kissed her on the cheek. "Happy birthday, Tarry. I still love you."

Tears again filled her eyes. He hadn't called her Tarry since they were little kids. He turned to leave, and she followed him to the door. He left and she leaned against it. He hurried to the elevator because he didn't want anyone to see him crying.

"Shoot! Why didn't I tell him to stay?" She threw open the door and sprinted after him, but it was too late. The elevator door closed. Caralyn ran back to her room and fell on the bed. She wept for a long time before sitting up. She walked into the bathroom, grabbed a tissue, wiped her face and then remembered her dress.

"Oh, crap! I hope I didn't ruin this dress." She took it off and smoothed out the wrinkles before hanging it back in the closet. She caressed the chiffon material and whispered, "I will only wear this for special occasions." She had just closed the closet door when the phone rang. She bounded to her desk, yanked her cell phone from her purse and answered before the second ring. "Oh, Bubby, I'm sorry," she cried.

"Who's Bubby?" Jeremiah asked.

"Someone special," she answered.

Check out these other titles by the author. Visit the website:
kennethleemcgee.com

The Emmy's Story Series

1. We Were 'posed to Get Married
2. One Of The Guys
3. A New Friend
4. Did You Like the Ravioli Tonight?
5. Completely and Forever: A Wedding
6. It's Time To Go!
7. How Difficult Can It Be?
8. Forever... Isabella... Forever
9. The Forgettable Year
10. Turning Thirty
11. Hello, I'm James
12. Remember The Struggle
13. But God! I Write Songs
14. A Lifelong Dream
15. Gideon's Tree
16. New Priorities
17. Christmas Surprise

The Annie Mercer O'Dell Series

1. Roosevelt High
2. North Park College
3. Smoky Mountain Summer

The Rex Ford & Clay Horn Books

1. The Amazing Adventures Of Rex Ford & Clay Horn

Stand Alone Books

1. Growing Up In Kinmundy Junction
2. Grandpa, Lions and Kitty Cats: A Collection Of Short Stories For Children Of All Ages
3. The True Stories Of Ol' Melvin, Obadiah, Perkins MacGhee and other Characters